Memo from J H C Goatberger
To: Thos. Cropper, overseer

May I remind you of <u>Mother Ogg's Tales For Tiny Folk</u>, published against my better judgement? May I remind you of the story of 'The Little Man Who Grew Too Big'? I personally thought it was a charming tale until my wife started laughing. No more Mrs Ogg. This is final.

Memo from Thos. Cropper
To: J H C Goatberger, publisher

While you were at lunch a troll came round about the rent. He works for Mr Chrysoprase. He made me an offer I understood only too well, especially the bit about forcing my toes into my ears. He wishes to see you tomorrow. PS I have still not yet disposed of the unsolicited MS from Mrs Ogg.

Memo from J H C Goatberger
To: Thos. Cropper, overseer

I swore I'd never ask this: what is the nature of this manuscript?

Memo from Thos. Cropper
To: J H C Goatberger, publisher

It is penned on her usual assortment of old sugar bags
and bits of wrapping paper. Some of it is written in
chalk. It appears to be...well...the notes and jottings
of a countrywoman. You know the sort of things:
etiquette, advice to Young People, garden lore, the
language of flowers, recipes...

Memo from J H C Goatberger
To: Thos. Cropper, overseer

I would hesitate to listen to the language
of any flowers in the vicinity of Mrs Ogg.
Let me ask you this directly: is jelly
involved, and if so in what shape?

Memo from Thos. Cropper
To: J H C Goatberger, publisher

There appears to be very little jelly.

Memo from J H C Goatberger
To: Thos. Cropper, overseer

How do we stand on custard?

Memo from Thos. Cropper
To: J H C Goatberger, publisher

There is some custard. I have examined it in some
detail and it appears to be devoid of innuendo.

Memo from J H C Goatberger
To: Thos. Cropper, overseer

Oh, all right. Get one of the hacks to put in the
grammar, punctuation and spelling, and make sure
it has pretty pictures. That's what people want.
Please also make sure that the manuscript is read
by my wife, who I have to say shows a disturbing
talent for working out what it is that Mrs Ogg is
getting up to. She keeps on threatening to make a
Strawberry Wobbler again. Perhaps this will take
her mind off it.

Memo from Thos. Cropper
To: J H C Goatberger, publisher

Some elements of Mrs Ogg's manuscript have caused me
concern. My suspicions were first aroused when I
identified large areas of text which seemed both
familiar and properly punctuated. A visit to the library
confirmed them. In short, sir, Mrs Ogg seems to believe
that writing a book largely involves copying things out
of other books and pasting them onto any bits of plain
paper she can find, then signing them 'G. Ogg' in crayon.
So far I have identified passages that bear considerable
resemblance to parts of:

Ankh-Morpork Almanack and Booke of Dayes
   (many of our back numbers)
Boots and Teeth
Ceremonies and Protocols of the Kingdom of Lancre
Lady Deirdre Waggon's Book of Etiquette
Gardening In Difficult Conditions
The Joy of Tantric Sex, with Illustrations for the
   Advanced Student
Toujours, Quirm
My Family and Other Werewolves
The Legendes and Antiquities of the Ramtops
The Country Dairy of a Gentlewoman (unbelievable!)
Twurp's Peerage
Wormold's Steerage

Memo from J H C Goatberger
To: Thos. Cropper, overseer

What the hell is Wormold's Steerage?

Memo from Thos. Cropper, overseer
To: J H C Goatberger

It was a sort of biographical dictionary of
all those people who would never, ever get
into Twurp's Peerage — renowned beggars,
champion Morris dancers, people who are
famous for the ability to make strange faces
or whistle through unconventional orifices,
and so on. It went out of print very quickly,
having failed to remember the most
important point about works of this nature,
viz., that the people in it should be rich
enough to be able to afford to buy copies.

Memo from J H C Goatberger
To: Thos. Cropper, overseer

You're telling me that Mrs Ogg has simply
recycled bits of more than a dozen books?

Memo from Thos. Cropper, overseer
To: J H C Goatberger

In a word, yes.

Memo from J H C Goatberger
To: Thos. Cropper, overseer

The cunning old biddy! Then it counts as
research and is perfectly OK. Don't worry
about it.

NANNY OGG'S
COOKBOOK

BY THE SAME AUTHOR:

The Joye of Snacks (banned)

Mother Ogg's Tales for Tiny Folk (withdrawn)

NANNY OGG'S COOKBOOK

INCLUDING RECIPES, ITEMS of Antiquarian Lore, Improving Observations of Life, Good Advice for Young People on the Threshold of the Adventure That is Marriage, Notes on Etiquette & Many Other Helpful Observations that will Not Offend the Most Delicate Sensibilities.

CORGI BOOKS

PRINTING HISTORY
Doubleday edition published 1999
Corgi edition published 2001

25

Copyright © Terry Pratchett and Stephen Briggs 1999
Illustrations © Paul Kidby
Recipes © Tina Hannan and Stephen Briggs

The right of Terry Pratchett and Stephen Briggs to be identified as the authors of this work has been asserted in accordance with sections 77 and 78 of the Copyright Designs and Patents Act 1988.

Typeset 11 on 15pt Class Garamond by Julia Lloyd.

Corgi Books are published by Transworld Publishers,
61–63 Uxbridge Road, London W5 5SA,
a division of The Random House Group Ltd,
in Australia by Random House Australia (Pty) Ltd,
20 Alfred Street, Milsons Point, Sydney, NSW 2061, Australia,
in New Zealand by Random House New Zealand Ltd,
18 Poland Road, Glenfield, Auckland 10, New Zealand
and in South Africa by Random House (Pty) Ltd,
Isle of Houghton, Corner of Boundary Road & Carse O'Gowrie,
Houghton 2198, South Africa

Penguin Random House is committed to a sustainable future for our business, our readers and our planet. This book is made from Forest Stewardship Council® certified paper.

Printed and bound in Great Britain by Clays Ltd, St Ives plc

CONTENTS

NOTES ABOUT Other Species—Rules of Precedence—Modes of Address—Etiquette
at the Table—Smoking—Some Notes on Gardening—Births—Courtship—
Balls—The Language of Flowers—Marriage—Death—Royal Occasions—
Etiquette in the Bedroom

PREFACE

by

THE AUTHOR

NOT A DAY goes past but I'm glad I was born in Lancre. I know every inch of the place and every one of the people an' I look out over its mountains, hills, woods and valleys and I think: 'That young couple have been in that spinney rather a long time, I shall have to have a word with her mam.'

But a lot of the old ways I knew when I was a girl are passin' now. There's six oil lamps in the kingdom to my knowledge, and up at the castle they put in one of them privies that cleans 'emselves, so instead of having to dig out the pit every week my lad Shawn, who does all the jobs up there apart from kinging, now merely has to fill up the 200-gallon tank on top of the tower. That is Progress for you. Of course it all ends up in the river so what you gains in convenience you loses in compost.

All this means that these are changin' times, and that's when people go around bewildered and full of uncertainty and they turn to me, because I am a *grande dame*, or 'big woman' as we would say here, and ask me the questions that is puzzling them, viz., if you are givin' a dinner party, what are the issues of etiquette involved in seatin' the man who makes a living putting weasels down his trousers at fairs, and who is therefore quite respected in these parts, next to the daughter of a man who once mugged the second son of an earl? Which is the kind of knotty problem a society hostess has to face every day, and it takes Experience not only to get it right but also to make sure there's a really soft cushion on the weasel juggler's chair, since the poor man suffers for his Art.

They ask me things like: what is the right way to address a duke? An' once again I have to point out that it is a matter of fine details, such as, if there's a gate needs holdin' open and it looks like half a dollar might be forthcoming, it's 'G'day, your graciousness,' whereas if you've just set fire to his ancestral piles and the mob is breakin' the windows it is more suitable to address him as 'you bloated lying blutocat!' It is all a matter of *finesse*.

People are coming to me all the time to ask things like, what kind of wedding anniversary d'you call it after ten years, or, is it lucky to plant beans on a Thursday. Of course, it is nat'ral for people to ask witches this sort of thing on account of us bein' the suppositories of tradition, but the younger girls I see around don't seem very keen on picking this sort of thing up, them being far too keen on candles and lucky crystals and so on. I reckon if a crystal's so lucky, how come it's ended up as a bit of rock? I don't trust all this occult, you never know who had it last.

Anyway, there's a lot more writin' around these days than there was when I was young and I thought, I will write down some of those little hints and tips which can smooth the lumpy bits on the pathway that is life. I've gone heavy on the recipes, because so much in life revolves around food. In fact good manners started to happen as soon as all the mammoths were killed off and there was no piece of food big enough for everyone to eat at the same time. A good meal is good manners.

G. Ogg

A NOTE

from

THE EDITORS

GYTHA 'NANNY' OGG, the author of these works, is a renowned practitioner of that combination of practical psychology, common sense and occult engineering known as witchcraft.

Her genius even extends to the written language, since it will be obvious to our readers that she has an approach to grammar and spelling that is all her very own. As far as punctuation goes she appears to have no approach at all, but seems merely to throw it at the page from a distance, like playing darts.

We have taken the liberty of smoothing out some of the more rumpled sentences while leaving, we hope, some flavour of the original. And, on that subject, we need to make a point about the weights and measures used in the cookery recipes. We have, reluctantly, translated them into metric terms because Nanny Ogg used throughout the very specialized unit of measure known as the 'some' (as in 'Take some flour and some sugar').

This required some, hah, experiment, because the 'some' is a unit of some, you see, complexity. Some flour is almost certainly more than some salt, but there appears to be no such thing as half of some, although there was the occasional mention of a 'bit' as in 'a bit of pepper'.

Instinctively, one feels that a bit of flour is more than some pepper but probably less than a bit of butter, and that a wodge of bread is probably about a handful, but we have found no reliable way of measuring a gnat's.

Timing also presented a problem, because Mrs Ogg has a very vague attitude to lengths except in humorously anatomical areas. We have not been able to come up with a reliable length of time equivalent to a 'while', which is an exponential measurement – one editor considered on empirical evidence that a 'while' in cookery was about 35 minutes, but we found several usages elsewhere of 'quite a while' extending up to ten years, which is a bit long for batter to stand. 'As long as it takes to sing "Where Has All The Custard Gone?"' looked helpful, but we haven't been able to find the words, so we have had to resort to boring old minutes.

Finally, there is the question of verisimilitude. In many of the recipes we have had to tinker with ingredients to allow for the fact that the Discworld equivalents are unavailable, inedible, or worse. Few authors can make a long-term living out of poisoning their readers, at least physically. Take the case of the various types of dwarf bread, for example. Brick dust, in Great Britain, is not generally found even in sausages. It's hard on the teeth. Granite is seldom served to humans. The biblical injunction that 'Man must eat a peck* of dirt before he dies' did not suggest that this was supposed to happen on just one plate. Also, most human food with the possible exception of the custard pie has never been designed for offensive purposes.

So, we have to say, strict accuracy has been sacrificed in the

* About nine litres dry measure, we're afraid.

interests of having as many readers at the end of this book as we had at the start. The aim has been to get the look and feel of the original Discworld recipes while avoiding, as far as possible, the original taste.

Terry Pratchett
Stephen Briggs

NANNY OGG'S
PHILOSOPHY
of
COOKERY

THEY SAY THAT the way to a man's heart is through his stomach, which just goes to show they're as confused about anatomy as they gen'rally are about everything else, unless they're talking about instructions on how to stab him, in which case a better way is up and under the ribcage.

Anyway, we do not live in a perfect world and it is foresighted and useful for a young woman to become proficient at those arts which will keep a weak-willed man from straying. Learning to cook is also useful (just my little joke, no offence meant!).

People say that proper housewifery has died out. They say the skills which once were taken for granted at all levels of society are being neglected because these days all everyone thinks about is pleasure – the theatre, reading, ball games, and, of course, making your own entertainment, which we never had time for when I was young.

My own granny even knew how to make sparrow pie when times were hard (a bit on the crunchy side, since you ask) but, nowadays, even if you gave a whole pig to half the housewives in these parts there would be, when they'd finished with it, *some bits left over*! My granny would have had to go and lie down.

Somehow the idea crept in that housework was not *real*. Well, I remember my mam's kitchen, all full of things bubbling, rising, pickling, soaking, salting and dripping. That smelled real, all right. As she said, any fool could earn sixpence a week working for Mr Poorchick, but it took real effort to make that stretch over nine children. If you want to know why country men set such score by growing fat pigs, huge pumpkins, giant marrows and parsnips you could use as fence posts, it was because they were big enough to go round. Never mind the vitamins and minerals, what you really wanted to get on your plate was lots.

Now I'm hearing where people in Ankh-Morpork are talking about 'the correct diet'. But the people doing the talking are mostly men. I've got nothing against men. Quite the contrary. But they can't *cook*. Oh, they can *cuisine* like no one's business. Put them in some huge kitchen with dozens of chefs and skivvies to shout at and they can manage to fry an egg and arrange it delicately on the plate with sprigs of this and that on a bed of somethin' vaguely sinister, but ask them to serve up meals every day to a huge bunch of hungry kids on a budget of sixpence and they'll have a bit of a headache. I daresay there are men who can manage it, but usually when I hear someone say that a husband cooks, I generally reckon it means he's got a recipe for something expensive and he does it twice a year. And then leaves the pans in the sink 'to soak'.

Now, I am an old wife, so when it comes to old wives' tales I know what I'm talking about. One of them is that good cookery only happens in the houses of the rich and well-bred. This is silly. There's more to good food than measuring the distance between your knife and fork, carving swans out of butter, and a salt cellar that looks like a scaled-down model of the Battle of Pseudopolis in solid silver – it's all in the selection of good-quality ingredients and the fact that there should be plenty of them. Don't talk to me about gold plates – if you can see what the plate is made of the portions are too small.

The time is ripe for a book with good, honest recipes for normal folk. Mind you, it isn't cookery books that are needed half so much as cooks who know what they are doing and can make a meal out of anything. That's why Genuan and Agatean cookery is all the rage in the cities now – *they* started out in places where all the good grub was pinched by other people and you had to find a way of eatin' things you normally wouldn't even want to look at. No one is going to learn how to make shark's fin soup because they *want* to.

But why should we turn our backs on good, honest Lancre and Sto Plains cuisine? It's just as good as food anywhere else on the Disc and I should know coz I've been there and tried it. Even if there are better cooking methods in foreign parts (and I don't necessarily say that there are) why should the good folk of Sto Helit, Scrote, Razorback and Bad Ass put up with food that's mostly boiled and the only herb you ever see is sage?

The simple routines of food preparation, the smells of food cooking – fryin' onions, apple pie with cloves, roasting beef – are all a part of the pleasure of eating. Of course, it's all the better if you're not doing the actual work. I've got a lot of daughters and daughters-in-law now, and they all live really close, and I've generally encouraged the view that a good plateful should always be sent round to Nanny. No one can say I'm not prepared to go that extra meal. And they're all good cooks, because I trained 'em well and I'd be sure to tell them if they wasn't.

One of the things that's slowed the advancement of good cooking is that cooks traditionally are very secretive about their recipes. They're handed down through families but guarded jealously against outsiders. I'm very pleased that, with a lot of help, we've got recipes from all over the Disc – from Mrs Colon, wife to Sergeant Fred Colon of the Ankh-Morpork City Watch, from Mustrum Ridcully, Archchancellor of Unseen University, from our own king, Verence II of Lancre. And many others. It's amazing what you can do with a little charm and a lot of blackmail.

It's hard to know exactly what category these recipes fall in 'specially since some of them barely count as food, but I've done my best to put them in order as First Courses, Main Dishes, Misc. Savouries (and some are very misc.), Pudding and Misc. Sweets. Dwarf cookery deserves a place of its own, probably as a boat anchor.

Let's start with the first course that could so easily become a last course if it's not done properly...

THE RECIPES

Deep-Sea Blowfish

(The Easy Version – not requiring years of training)

SERVES 2 AS A STARTER

1 deep-sea blowfish
50g sea bream or other white fish,
  absolutely fresh, filleted
3—4 radishes
2—3 spring onions
a few sprigs of watercress

an eggcup full of light soy sauce
  to use as a dip, mixed with:
1 teaspoon mustard or
2 teaspoons lemon juice or
1 clove garlic, crushed

THE MOST IMPORTANT thing here is *not to use any of the blowfish whatsoever*, since every single part of it is deadly in a very unpleasant way. Basic'ly, they'd be able to bury you in an envelope. So, after covering all work surfaces, dispose of the blowfish very carefully. Better yet, get someone else, perhaps someone you don't like very much but who doesn't owe you any money, to dispose of the blowfish. An incinerator would be an ideal place, provided the smoke is blowing in the direction of unnecessary people.

Of course, you might ask why bother to obtain a deep-sea blowfish at all? Well, if you do not, the dish will still be very pleasant. But it will not have that delicate *frisson*, as they call it, which lifts the dish to gastronomic heaven. Connoisseurs claim they can tell by the taste if a blowfish has been anywhere near the kitchen on the day of preparation, and woe betide the chef who just couldn't be bothered to go out

and buy one. They say the dish knows there's been a blowfish nearby.

I heard where some wizards reckon that the blowfish business is a bit like that idea that water *remembers what's been in it*. That's pretty clever. But when you think of some of the things that people have put in water, and then remember that water goes round and round again, maybe it's best to drink beer.

My feelin' is that people know the dish is a genuine blowfish dish when they've been charged $100 for it. If some food wasn't so expensive, no one would eat it.

Since blowfish are so very expensive, perhaps you'd just better settle for the rest of the recipe:

Check the fish for any scales or bones and remove any you find. Place in a colander and quickly pour boiling water over it, then immediately plunge the fish into a bowl of cold water; the object is not to cook it but to make sure it is clean.

Finely slice the radishes and spring onion (lengthways) and arrange into pretty patterns on two plates, along with the watercress. Using a very sharp knife, carefully slice the fish as thinly as possible. Serve immediately, with the soy dip.

Bananana Soup Surprise

People say: 'What's so surprisin' about bananana soup?' And I say, it's got banananas in it. Of course, if you've ever read my book *The Joye of Snacks* you'll spot that some of my *special* ingredients have been left out. People complained they made the soup a bit *too* surprisin'.

SERVES 4

4 large banananas, peeled
470ml vegetable stock
155ml dry sherry
1 heaped teaspoon ground nutmeg

1 heaped teaspoon brown sugar
2 heaped teaspoons chopped chervil
pinch of salt and pepper
1 teaspoon lemon juice

CHOP TWO OF the banananas and put into a pan with the stock. Blend or mash until the banananas are smooth and well, er, blended. Slowly bring the liquid to simmering point, taking care not to let it boil, and add the remaining ingredients. Stir gently for 2–3 minutes to ensure that all the sugar has dissolved and leave to simmer for a further 5 minutes, stirring frequently.

Take the remaining two banananas and chop them in half widthways. Place each half in a bowl, pointing upwards. Pour in some soup and serve.

Surprisin', eh?

Celery Astonishment

All right, it's not that astonishing. They wouldn't let me add all the inter-estin' bits, especially the aubergine. They said someone's wife laughed. I just think mealtimes should be amusing. That's my opinion.

SERVES 2

1 large head of celery
300g cooked rice
1 green pepper, seeded
and chopped
3 tomatoes, chopped

60g grated Parmesan cheese
1 teaspoon lemon juice
1 tablespoon chopped tarragon
1 egg, beaten
salt and pepper

PREHEAT THE OVEN to 200°C/Gas 6. Prepare the celery by carefully removing the inner stalks, any leaves, mud, etc., to form a hollow. Mix together all the remaining ingre-dients except the egg, and check seasoning. Bind together with the egg.

Take a large piece of lightly oiled cooking foil and place it on a baking tray. Place the celery on the foil and stuff it with the mix-ture. Tie with string around the loose ends to prevent the stuffing falling out, wrap in the foil, and bake in the oven for 1½–2 hours until celery is tender.

To serve, carefully unwrap and place on an oval serving platter with two judiciously placed baked potatoes mayhap. Carve at the table.

Primal Soup

A popular dish at Unseen University and, it is rumoured, among the gods themselves. It is said to be the soup from which all life evolved, and if you leave this one long enough life will definitely evolve in it.*

SERVES 4 AS A MAIN COURSE OR 6 AS A STARTER

470ml fish stock

50g salmon, filleted and skinned

50g cod, filleted and skinned

12 mussels, shelled and cleaned

50g crab meat (prepared) or 4 crab sticks, roughly shredded

6–10 baby octopus tentacles, cleaned

230g tin chopped tomatoes

150ml dry white wine

2–3 cloves garlic, crushed

1 tablespoon roughly chopped parsley

1 tablespoon chopped dill

1 teaspoon paprika

2 vermicelli nests (approx. 25g each)

100g shrimps, shelled and cooked

a few drops gravy browning/green food dye (optional)

1 large egg, beaten

salt and pepper

HEAT THE FISH stock in a large pan. Roughly chop the salmon and cod and drop into the stock.

Simmer on a gentle heat until the fish is nearly cooked. Then remove from the heat and stir until the fish chunks separate and break down. Return to the heat and add the mussels, crab meat and tentacles. Bring to a simmer. Add the tomatoes and wine and return to a low heat. Add the herbs, garlic and seasonings, the vermicelli and shrimps, and simmer until the pasta cooks. Add browning/food dye if required, and check seasoning. Finally, add the egg and gently stir until cooked. Then quickly bring the mixture to the boil for a few seconds and serve.

*Technically (see *The Science of Discworld*), primal soup should be a vivid turquoise. But no one who is anyone was there, so why worry?

Bread and Water

(Kindly donated by Lord Vetinari, Patrician of Ankh-Morpork)

3 whole, freshly baked loaves   *1 flagon freshly drawn water*

HOWEVER EFFICIENT A ruler may be, there is always someone, isn't there, who feels that his diet might be improved by some artificial additive, such as arsenic. Many rulers have sought ways to avoid this. This is one classical method:

Have sufficient dough made to make three loaves of bread. Bake the resulting loaves in an oven. Both these operations should be supervised by at least two reliable employees.

Select one of the three loaves (the other two must be eaten by the baker). Slice it. Select slices at random and have these tested in your presence by members of the Palace staff (or members of your family if you are not fortunate enough to live in a palace). From the remaining slices select one; place this on a plate selected at random from the kitchens. Have the remaining plates licked by the kitchen staff; pause to observe any negative reactions to this operation, or to the earlier slice-testing.

In the meantime, have a bucket of water drawn from the well. Have this boiled, poured into a flagon and cooled. From this flagon pour four glasses of water. Select three at random and have them drunk by different members of the Palace staff from those who are testing the bread/plates.

You might now believe that you have a glass of water and some slices of bread that are free of poison, in which case you have failed to grasp the situation. There are such things as antidotes, which even a trainee poisoner will have taken as a precautionary measure. And then of course there was the case of Lord Samphire: the bread passed the test, and so did the water. The problem came to light only if you ate the bread and *then* drank the water.

Here is my preferred method, which has stood me in good stead.

1 Arrange the politics of the country over a period of years so that poisoning you will be more trouble than it is worth and interfere with the private ambitions of too many people just at the moment.
2 Make sure that there are among the city's civil service some unpredictable men who will consider your poisoning a personal insult against them, and generally cause a lot of fuss.
3 Then eat what you please.

Mrs Colon's Genyooin Klatchian Curry

A note from the editors: Few recipes in these pages have caused so much debate as this one. Anyone over the age of forty knows how the classic recipe goes, because it has been invented and reinvented thousands of times by ladies who have heard about foreign parts but have no wish to bite into them.

Its mere existence is a telling argument for a liberal immigration policy.

Like real curry, it includes any ingredients that are to hand. The resemblance stops there, however. It *must* use bright green peas, lumps of swede and, for the connoisseur of gastronomic history, watery slivers of turnip. For wateriness is the *key* to this curry; its 'sauce' should be very thin and of an unpleasant if familiar colour. And it must use a very small amount of 'curry powder', a substance totally unknown in those areas where curry grows naturally, as it were; sometimes it's enough just to take the unopened tin out of the pantry and wave it vaguely over the pan. Oh, and remember that the sultanas must be yellow and swollen. And soggy. And sort of gritty, too (ah, you remember . . .)

Last-minute warning: This recipe has been changed slightly in order to make it quite nice really. Well, better than the real thing, anyway. A lot better, come to think of it. Foreigner-free curry is probably the nearest most humans get to the philosophy behind dwarf bread; the mere *thought* of it makes you prepared to eat almost anything else.

SERVES 4

2 tablespoons sunflower oil
1 large onion, roughly chopped
2 cloves garlic, chopped
225g broccoli florets
1 red pepper, seeded and chopped
1 green pepper, seeded and chopped

350g swede, chopped and boiled
   until just tender
225g peas (frozen will be fine)
50g raisins or sultanas
1 teaspoon each of ground ginger,
   cumin and coriander

1 teaspoon curry powder (optional, for old time's sake)
½ teaspoon ground turmeric
175ml coconut milk

250ml vegetable stock
tomato purée to thicken, if needed
2 teaspoons brown mustard seeds
salt and black pepper

PREHEAT THE OVEN to 180°C/Gas 4. Heat the oil in a large frying pan. Add the onion, garlic, broccoli, peppers and cook until the onion starts to soften. Then add the part-cooked swede, the peas and raisins and cook gently for a further 5 minutes. Add the spices (but not the mustard seeds), the coconut milk and about half the vegetable stock. Cook for a further 10 minutes or so, adding extra stock if the mixture needs it. If it seems too runny, add a little tomato purée to thicken.

Transfer the mixture to a casserole dish, season, sprinkle with the mustard seeds, cover and cook in the oven for about 45 minutes. Serve with rice or nan bread. Run away.

Sergeant Fred Colon of Ankh-Morpork City Watch is a man known to be against 'anything foreign' in all walks of life. This curry, devised by his wife, is one of a range of special 'morporkified' Colon dishes that include the Fish 'n' Chip Pizza, Fried Sushi and smorgasbord with the tops on.

Sheep's Eyes

Everyone knows they eat sheep's eyes in Klatch, but no one reports actually seeing them doin' it.* I call this suspicious. Oh, *yes*, they offer them to *guests*. I bet if I lived in a desert I'd do anything for a laugh, too. This recipe is, er, restored. That is, it's a complete fake. But it's a lot more edible.

eyeball-sized pickled onions (as many as you wish to make)

stuffed green olives
tube of cream cheese

CAREFULLY REMOVE THE inside of each onion, taking care to leave the outer skins intact except for a hole at either end. (*Note:* one of the holes must be big enough to have an olive pushed through it.) Half fill the skin with cream cheese and then insert an olive, making sure that the stuffing is visible . . . some of the cheese should squirt out of the other end, making a 'tail'. If it doesn't, squirt in more until it does!

*See *Jingo* for the correct etiquette when offered sheep's eyes.

Slumpie

Your classic Sto Plains Slumpie, one of Ankh-Morpork's most famous dishes, is one of your stick-to-the-ribs meals, 'cos there's times when it's too cold for any of that fancy vitamin stuff. Technic'ly, Slumpie should have vast amounts of mashed-up elderly potatoes and swedes, with a big knob of butter to help 'em, but Slumpie is a bit like *chop suey*, which is Agatean for 'all the labels have fallen off the tins', and you can make it out of more or less anything so long as you call it Slumpie. This one has got some actual flavour, and is designed as a main dish rather than as something to stop the meat falling off the plate.

SERVES 3–4

500g minced beef
1 tablespoon vegetable oil
3 cloves garlic, chopped
100g fresh mushrooms, sliced
470ml beef stock
470ml dark ale
375g frozen leaf spinach

1 tablespoon tomato purée
1 heaped teaspoon rubbed sage
1 heaped teaspoon English mustard
salt and pepper
60g butter and 60g flour, mixed to
   a smooth paste (optional; use, if
   required, to thicken the sauce)

BROWN THE MINCE in the oil with the garlic. Add the mushrooms, stock and ale and bring to the boil. Add the spinach and the rest of the ingredients and bring back to the boil. Simmer for about half an hour or until the liquid has reduced by about a quarter.

Serve with clooty dumplings (page 56), or with mash.

Rincewind's Potato Cakes

Note from the editors: We confess to some difficulty in getting a recipe out of Rincewind, one of Unseen University's best-known wizards. It involved a considerable amount of travel, much of it at high speed, since Rincewind's major talent is to run away from anything that is frightening and this, when you come to think of it, is a pretty good definition of the universe. The original suggestion, shouted over his shoulder, was 'Potatoes! Lots of potatoes! In their jackets! In great big baths of butter!'

This seemed to us to be too close to the Librarian's recipe (see page 80), although it uses a vegetable rather than a fruit (except that the potato is technically a nut). However, we understand that Rincewind has been so long away from the one thing that makes life worthwhile (potatoes) that he will eat *anything* if it has a potato in it.

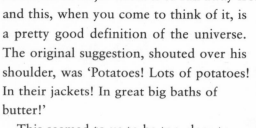

38

1 onion, chopped
350g potatoes, cooked and mashed
1 teaspoon sage

1 or 2 eggs, beaten
100g white breadcrumbs, dried
sunflower oil

Fry the onion in a little oil until softened. Stir into the mashed potato with the sage and allow the mixture to cool. Then form the mixture into patties, about the size and shape of small, thick beefburgers. Brush the patties with the beaten egg and then turn them in a bowl containing the breadcrumbs. Heat some more oil in a frying pan and fry the potato cakes until they are golden brown.

They are quite delicious and can be eaten on the run.

Lady Sybil Vimes's Kedgeree

I have to tell you that this should have been a recipe from Commander Vimes of Ankh-Morpork City Watch. He is a man who thinks that if it isn't fried it isn't really food, and the recipe would have been Pork Scratchings Cookies, which are a real treat for anyone whose favourite food group is Burnt Crunchy Bits.

However, Lady Sybil feels that since he's a Duke and a Sir and a couple of other things as well her husband should have more nobby* tastes, and there's nothing more nobby than those breakfasts where you have to lift three silver lids before you even find something you recognize. Even though he feels a bit of a class traitor, Commander Vimes agrees that there's nothing like a bit of early-morning haddock to build an empire.

I always say that if you've got a good breakfast inside you you can face anything the day has in store.

*Which is not the same as the same tastes as Nobby Nobbs, and *certainly* not the same as the taste of Nobby. Sometimes even my mind can boggle a bit.

150g long-grain rice

125ml milk

125ml water

450g smoked haddock

50g butter

1 tablespoon mild curry powder

2 hardboiled eggs, chopped

salt and pepper

ADD THE RICE to a saucepan of boiling salted water and cook until *al dente* (posh for one step away from being mushy) – about 15–20 minutes. Drain and rinse it, and leave in the strainer.

In a frying pan heat the milk and water to simmering point, add the fish and poach gently for about 5 minutes. Lift out the fish and carefully remove the skin and bones; break up the flesh into medium-sized pieces. Discard the cooking liquid.

Melt half the butter in the frying pan, blend in the curry powder, add the flaked fish and warm the mixture through. Remove from the heat and stir in the chopped eggs. Season with salt and pepper.

In a separate pan melt the remaining butter, add the rice and stir well to coat the grains. Season, then add this mixture to the fish and eggs. Mix well.

Serve on a warmed dish. Then go out and conquer a continent.

Fikkun Haddock

As my dad used to say, if you're goin' to have a haddock you don't want a fin'un. By the time they got all the way up to Lancre, in the mountains, the fish were high in more ways than one and a good cook would try all sorts of ideas to disguise the flavour, such as serving it in delicate sauces, often involving creosote, or, in the worst cases, wrapping it in lead foil and throwing it over a cliff. This one is for fish who aren't so far gone!

SERVES 3–4

30g butter
a dash of olive oil
1 medium onion, sliced
375g smoked haddock fillets
  (skins removed)
300ml fish stock

300ml dry cider
2—3 sprigs of tarragon, chopped
2—3 sprigs of chervil, chopped
1 tablespoon wholegrain mustard
salt and pepper

MELT THE BUTTER in a large pan with the olive oil, add the onion and sauté for around 5 minutes until softened, taking care not to burn it. Add the fish and cook for a couple of minutes on each side, then pour in the cider and enough of the stock to cover the fish. Add the remaining ingredients and stir gently. Bring to the boil, cover the pan and leave to simmer for a further 5 minutes. When the fillets start to break up, season to taste. No creosote need be used.

Genuine Howondaland Curry

(Taken from the writings of Ponce da Quirm)

Ponce da Quirm spent his whole life exploring foreign parts, I heard, and maybe it was because people laughed at his name.* Apparently he was looking for the Fountain of Youth and the odd thing about this sort of business is that it's never, ever close to. You'd think, on average, that *some* of these lost fountains of youth, trees of life and cities of gold would be really close, but they never are. And you never get people from a long way off coming to *our* part of the world lookin' for, as it might be, the Cottage of Doom or the Lost Chicken Shed.

Ponce brought back fourteen different kinds of plant and seven interestin' sorts of animal to this part of the world, but he insisted very firmly that none of them were named after him. That's how everyone remembers him.

This curry was one he made up durin' a period when he was shipwrecked on an island that had nothing but great big fat chickeny-birds that couldn't even fly. He did leave one, though, so's not to upset the balance of nature. Sometimes I reckon it would be better if there was a Fountain of Growing Up.

SERVES 4

4 chicken breasts, skinned and
   cut into cubes
small pot natural yoghurt
1cm piece of ginger root, grated
6—8 garlic cloves, crushed
2 tablespoons olive oil

1 large onion, chopped
4 fresh green chilli peppers, seeded and
   finely chopped
$^1/_2$ tablespoon ground cumin
$^1/_2$ tablespoon ground coriander
1 teaspoon turmeric

* See *Eric*.

1 400ml tin of coconut milk	salt to taste
water	fresh coriander leaves, chopped

Note: You could use a tin of tomatoes instead of the coconut milk, or liquidized cashew nuts.

MIX THE CHICKEN cubes in a bowl with the yoghurt, half the grated ginger and half the crushed garlic. Leave for at least half an hour, or, better, overnight.

Heat the oil in a large pan, and cook the chopped onion for about 10 minutes, stirring occasionally, until it is a definite brown. Some bits might be even dark brown – this changes the taste and makes the curry sweeter.

Stir in half the chillies, the remaining ginger and garlic, and the powdered spices. You should have a paste. Tip in the coconut milk and cook for about 8–10 minutes, or until the mixture starts to get really dry and the oil starts to come out (this shouldn't happen unless the heat is too high).

When it all looks thoroughly cooked and a nice thick sauce consistency, add the chicken and yoghurt mix, and a splash of water (about half a mug) and some salt. You could add a bit of lemon juice and a pinch of sugar if you want. Turn the heat down if it's higher than mediumish, and let it simmer away slowly for 15–30 minutes.

Just before the end (5 minutes) add chopped green chillies to taste. You can put chopped fresh coriander leaves on the top, if you like, for that authentic Howondaland restaurant look.

Eat with nan. In fact, invite all your relatives.

Carrot and Oyster Pie

Carrots so's you can see in the dark and oysters so's you've got something to look at, as I always say. I used to make this for the first Mr Ogg, and he never complained. Mind you, he never complained about anything very much.

Oysters are said to make you frisky. However, take a look at an oyster in a tank. Go back and look at it again a few hours later. Do you notice any changes? No. That's how full of beans oysters are. I'm told that the process of makin' oysters happens a long way from the oyster, and I can't see that catching on with humans.

Note: You could use fresh oysters (about 12) but, well, tinned are so much easier, and are available whenever there's a vowel in the month.

SERVES 2

85g tinned smoked oysters in oil
125g grated carrot
1 teaspoon chopped chervil
1 teaspoon chopped dill
155ml Chablis (or other dry white wine)

300ml fish stock
30g Stilton cheese
250g puff pastry

PREHEAT THE OVEN to 200°C/Gas 6. Mix the oysters and the carrot with the herbs in a small pie dish. Pour in the wine and enough of the stock to cover the ingredients. Crumble the Stilton over the mixture.

Roll out the pastry to about 1cm thickness and carefully cover the dish with it. Trim any excess pastry, make a small hole in the top to let the steam escape and bake in the top part of the oven for 25–30 minutes or until the pastry is well risen and golden brown.

Mrs Whitlow's Artery-Hardening Hogswatch Pie

This is the pie favoured by Mrs Whitlow, housekeeper at Unseen University, as a handy snack for wizards around the dark time of year. It may seem difficult to feed a lot of hungry wizards, but experience has taught her, she says, to put something large in front of them. It often doesn't matter much what it is.

However, it is a matter of pride to her that it should be something worthwhile. It is sometimes as long as two hours between meals at UU, and a senior wizard will definitely feel rather peckish. This is a good filler.

SERVES 8

FOR THE PASTRY

450g plain flour

1 teaspoon salt

100g lard

150ml water

4 tablespoons milk

FOR THE FILLING

225g lean pork, minced

225g cooked ham, finely chopped

1 small onion, finely chopped

¹/₂ teaspoon ground allspice

¹/₂ teaspoon ground nutmeg

1 teaspoon dried rubbed sage

350g cooked pork cocktail sausages

beaten egg, to glaze

2 teaspoons powdered gelatine

150ml hot ham stock

150ml port

salt and pepper

PREHEAT THE OVEN to 200°C/Gas 6. Grease a raised pie mould, 18–20cm round, or a 1kg loaf tin.

To make the pastry, sift the flour and salt into a mixing bowl. Put the lard, water and milk in a saucepan, stir over a medium heat until the lard is melted and then bring to the boil. Pour on to the flour and work into a pliable dough. Knead lightly. Roll out three-quarters of the pastry and use to line the greased pie mould or tin.

To make the filling, combine the pork, ham, onion, spices and sage in a bowl and season well with salt and pepper. Put half of this mixture in the base of the pie, cover with the whole cocktail sausages and then with the remaining minced pork mixture.

Roll out the remaining pastry for a lid (saving a little for decoration), and cut a small hole in the top. Dampen the pie's pastry edges, cover with the lid and press well together. Roll out the last bits of pastry and make sausage or pig shapes; arrange these on the top, finally brushing the whole with beaten egg. Bake in the oven for 30 minutes. Reduce the temperature and bake for a further $1^{1}/_{4}$ –$1^{1}/_{2}$ hours, covering the pie with greaseproof paper when it is sufficiently browned.

Dissolve the gelatine in the stock, season well and add the port. As the pie cools, pour the stock into the pie through a funnel inserted in the hole, tilting the pie to ensure that the stock is evenly distributed inside the pie.

Cool, then chill overnight until firm, before removing from the tin. Serve cut into slices.

Brodequin Rôti Façon Ombres

A bit of an odd one, this. It's foreign for 'Man's boots in mud'. They say that a posh restaurant in Ankh-Morpork ended up one day with nothing in its larder but mud and old boots and a restaurant full of people.* Now, some people might call this a tragedy, or at least a bit of a problem, but since the art of cuisine is to make something out of nothing and charge a lot of money for doing it, the chefs got cracking and produced such a range of delicacies that now old boots fetch quite a high price in the city and rare, sun-dried muds are imported from foreign parts.

This recipe has been adjusted to give the look but, I hope, not the taste.

SERVES 3–4

350g topside of beef, thinly sliced
3–4 tablespoons dark soy sauce
500g mushrooms, very finely chopped
300ml dark ale or stout

2 cloves garlic, crushed
2–3 teaspoons chopped dill
470ml beef stock
salt and pepper

MARINATE THE BEEF in the soy sauce for 2–3 hours. Preheat the oven to 190°C/Gas 5–6. Put the beef in a casserole dish with the mushrooms and add the ale. Add the garlic and dill and enough stock to cover. Season to taste. Cover and cook in the oven for $1^1/_2$ hours. Remove the lid and cook for a further 20–30 minutes to allow the 'mud' to reduce a little.

Note: The classic accompaniment, according to the Ankh-Morpork beggar, man about town and street gastrognome Arnold Sideways, is a rusty tin half filled with paint thinner. I would suggest something else. Practically anything else, really.

* See Hogfather.

Sergeant Angua's Vegetable Stew
with Dumplings

It's obviously very difficult for a werewolf livin' in a big city where you can't get what you're used to at home, such as people. In fact Sergeant Angua of the City Watch assures me she's never ate very much of anyone, and none of us can help the way we was brought up in any case. Of course, it's even harder if you're a *vegetarian* werewolf, because while that's okay by the human side there's no way you are going to persuade the wolf side to hunt down lentils. Cleaning your teeth in the morning can't be much fun when you've turned back into a human again, either.

A vegetarian werewolf is always looking for something different, and this is worth stayin' human for:

SERVES 4

1 tablespoon olive oil
450g leeks, sliced
1 green pepper, seeded and chopped
2 carrots, diced
3 cloves garlic, chopped
300g mushrooms, sliced

300ml vegetable stock
1 400g can chopped tomatoes
1 tablespoon paprika
1 400g can mixed beans
1 tablespoon balsamic vinegar
salt and pepper

FOR THE DUMPLINGS

125g self-raising flour
$^2/_3$ tablespoon mixed herbs
50g vegetable suet

4—5 tablespoons water
salt and pepper

HEAT THE OIL in a large frying pan and cook the leeks, green pepper, carrot and garlic for a few minutes. Add the mushrooms and cook for another few minutes. Add the vegetable stock, the tomatoes and the paprika. Bring to the boil and then simmer for 15–20 minutes.

Meanwhile, make the dumplings: mix together all the ingredients and then divide the mixture into a dozen pieces, shaping each into a ball.

Add the beans and the balsamic vinegar to the stew, and season. Place the dumplings on the surface, cover and simmer for 20–25 minutes. Good at any phase of the moon.

Mrs Gogol's Clairvoyant Gumbo

Gumbo is one of those dishes, like stew, where it's ridiculous to have a recipe. You just make it. And you can prob'ly make gumbo of a sort by simply dredging a swamp and boilin' up everything that tries to climb out of the net. But it won't be anything like Mrs Gogol's gumbo. Mrs Gogol* is a witch over in the swamps around Genua, where the magic's more into stickin' pins in people and turnin' people into zombies, and there's prob'ly some magic in the cookery, too.

Mrs Gogol says she can see the future in her gumbo. You need the knack. But the future you'll see in this one contains a good dinner at least.

SERVES 6

3 tablespoons olive oil

3 heaped tablespoons flour
  (for the roux)

2 large (or 3 small) celery stalks,
  trimmed and finely chopped

1 small green pepper, seeded
  and chopped

1 small red onion, chopped

2–3 heaped tablespoons Genuan
  spice mix (see page 53)

470ml fish stock (or chicken, or veg)

400g tin chopped tomatoes

10–12 pieces okra, chopped

* See *Witches Abroad*.

1 tablespoon dried basil
1 tablespoon dried oregano
1 tablespoon dried parsley
salt
8—10 drops hot pepper sauce
$^1/_2$ tablespoon Worcestershire sauce

100ml bourbon (or whisky will do)
meat from 1 large prepared crab
  (or 4 small whole ones)
600g ready-peeled prawns (or 650g
  in shells)

HEAT THE OIL in a saucepan and stir in the flour. Cook for about 5 minutes (medium heat), stirring, until it turns golden brown. Add the celery, pepper and onion and fry until softened. Add the Genuan spice mix and stir for another minute. Pour in the stock, stir well to ensure there are no lumps and then add the remaining ingredients except the crab and prawns. Leave to simmer, stirring occasionally, for 20 minutes. Add the crab meat and prawns, turn the heat up and bring to boiling point, then turn back down to medium and cook for a further 8–10 minutes (10–15 minutes if using crabs/prawns in shells).

Serve with rice.

Note: The Genuan spice mix and hot pepper sauce will make a hot gumbo. Use less if you're not used to spicy food.

C.M.O.T. Dibbler's Sausage Inna Bun

No visit to Ankh-Morpork is complete without a taste of one of Mr Cut-Me-Own-Throat Dibbler's famous pies or sausages-in-a-bun. Then it is sometimes completed very, very quickly. The amazin' thing is, though, that people will go back and try them again. I suppose it's because they want to check that their memory isn't playin' tricks on them. Mr Dibbler has kindly contributed this recipe.

MAKES ABOUT 30 SAUSAGES

1.4kg top-quality pork, minced* $^1/_2$ teaspoon ground nutmeg
450g breadcrumbs   water
1 teaspoon black pepper   sausage skins
3 tablespoons chopped fresh sage   buns of your choice

MIX ALL THE sausage ingredients in a bowl. Add enough water to achieve a nice, squidgy texture and fill the sausage skins with the result. Twist into links.

Grill or fry and serve hot in freshly baked buns.

*Note from Mr Dibbler: I always use good-quality pork, with about two-thirds lean meat to one-third fat. I insist that any skin, gristle or other dubious parts of the beast are excluded from the mixture.†

†This is what he says, and I for one believe it. It is not good etiquette to look at one of his sausages and say 'woof woof!' or 'neighhh!'

Nanny Ogg's Special Nibbles
with Special Party Dip, Made Specially

They don't have parties like they had when I was young . . . you know, with jelly and ice cream and you were sick with excitement before you got home.

I've been told I shouldn't put too many suggestive recipes in this book, although to my mind things are only suggestive if you're open to suggestions (for example, my friend Esmerelda Weatherwax thought the maypole was just a nice country custom until someone explained symbolism to her, and I just *don't* want to be there if anyone tells her about broomsticks). Anyway, tomatoes is considered aphrodisiacal, and my grandson Shane who is a sailor and has seen a thing or two says so is a bananana. Surprisin'ly enough, it gives a nice flavour to the dip.

FOR THE DIP

1 small onion
1 firm, just-ripe bananana
1 small cucumber (or half a large one)
1 400g can love apples (chopped tomatoes)

1 tablespoon chopped fresh coriander
2 teaspoons chopped fresh chilli or chilli powder
3 cloves garlic, crushed
salt and lemon juice, to taste

FOR THE NIBBLES

3 pitta breads
1 tablespoon Genuan spice mix (see opposite)

olive oil

TO MAKE THE dip: finely chop the onion, bananana and cucumber and mix with the remaining ingredients. Chill for at least an hour.

To make the nibbles: preheat the oven to 180°C/Gas 4. Mix the spice mix with enough oil to make a runny paste. Slit the pitta breads in half lengthways to form two thin pieces and cut (scissors are best) into a variety of interesting and appealing shapes. Place on a baking tray (do not overlap them) and brush lightly with the oil/spice mix. Bake for 8–10 minutes, or until golden brown and crispy.

Genuan Spice Mix

1 tablespoon hot paprika
1 tablespoon onion powder
1 tablespoon garlic powder

1 teaspoon chilli powder
$^1/_2$ tablespoon salt
2 teaspoons dried mixed herbs

Mix all the ingredients together and store in an airtight container. The adventurous can also try this mix on banged grains.

Leonard of Quirm's Recipe for a Cheese Sandwich

(Contributed by that remarkable if somewhat absent-minded genius)

Decide that shape of common loaf is not suitable for the purpose. Design new baking tin. Devise a new method of soldering tin. Design more efficient oven.

Doodle in margins a war engine for overcoming all obstacles and firing gouts of unquenchable fire on to enemy soldiers.

Design a new type of harrow. Convert war engine into a device for hauling ploughs and other agricultural implements over any kind of terrain no matter how rough. Since its traction is its key feature, decide to call it a Machine for Pulling Heavy Loads.

Convert old design for an improved fighting machine into a better flail. In the margin draw a small picture of a hand.

Design breadknife. Design machine for making breadknives. Design an improved wheel bearing, using small balls of, e.g., steel. Design shot tower for making steel balls of any size. Devise a small hand-cranked machine by which bread of any size and thickness can be smoothly buttered to any depth.

Consider designs of milk churns, and improve them. Hear that temperature regulation in dairies is vitally important in the manufacture of good cheese; design a device for regulating temperature by means of expanding metal strips, coupled to pulleys. Call it the Device for Regulating Temperature by Means of Metal Strips (Coupled to Pulleys).

Design instrument for waging war over a great distance by focusing the rays of the sun, and then adapt this to the oven design. Adapt inexplicably non-working machine for flying and turn into a novel device for churning butter by means of a wind-

mill. With a small adapter this can, in times of war, easily become
a device for hurling balls of burning butter for up to half a mile.

Design a device by which the moon can be reached, powered by
eggs.

Send out for pizza.

Clooty Dumplings

I've always been famous for my dumplings. Ask anyone. But the days of the giant, family-sized dumpling boiled up in a 'clooty' or 'motheaten old vest' seem to have passed. People just don't seem to have time to spend in sitting very still to digest their food any more, they want to be up and walking around within a few hours of lunch. So these belong to a different age, and recreating them is like bringing a dinosaur back to life. But they're much better than you might think; making a good dumpling is a mark of a skilled cook. You'll find that out if ever you have to eat one made by a bad cook.

These have been adjusted a little to take account of the modern taste for finicky food. Serve with Slumpie (page 37).

MAKES 4 LARGE ONES

100g wholemeal flour
50g chopped suet
1 heaped teaspoon wholegrain mustard
salt and pepper

3—4 tablespoons water
large pan of stock (vegetable, beef, chicken — whatever suits your guests)

MIX THE FLOUR and suet, making sure there are no lumps. Add the mustard and a little salt and pepper and mix well. Add just enough water to make a stiff paste. Break into four equal pieces and roll into balls.

Bring the stock to the boil. Carefully drop in the dumplings and simmer for 10–15 minutes. They should slide off a knife pushed through their centres when done. If the knife bends, you have done something wrong.

Clammers Beefymite Spread

My grandson Shane came across Clammers Beefymite Spread in a shop in Ankh-Morpork and got a bit partial to it. I wrote to that Mr Clammer, y'know, as one cook to another, offering to swap the recipe for my special version of Strawberry Wobbler for his beefymite, but he wasn't having none of it. So I've had to produce my own, which Shane likes just as much and it's a) a lot cheaper than havin' it shipped all the way from Ankh-Morpork, b) nothing like the real thing, c) completely different and d) tasty.

340g corned beef
2 tablespoons Worcestershire sauce
3 tablespoons mushroom ketchup

$^1/_4$–$^1/_2$ level teaspoon cayenne pepper
4–5 drops gravy browning (optional)

MIX THE INGREDIENTS to a smooth paste in a blender – or use a potato masher or fork. Transfer to clean jamjars or other sealable containers. Best eaten within 3–4 days. Store in the fridge.

GET THEE SPOON
OUT OF THEE JAR,
3 TRIES
FOR A PENNY!!!

Wow-Wow Sauce

A note from the editors: We offer no apologies for including this; it has proved very popular.

The recipe for Wow-Wow Sauce is a hereditary possession of the Ridcully family. Archchancellor Ridcully, like most wizards, is a man who goes for sauces; if you are the kind of person who takes a beefy patty between two halves of a bun and then covers it with cheese, and a pickle, and some green relish, and some red relish, and a different sort of pickle, and then some dark mustard, not forgetting of course some light mustard, and then some bits of green and other things until the meat slides out unnoticed and falls onto the floor, then you are of a magical inclination. A wizard will lick the top of a sauce bottle if he thinks no one is watching.

This is of course not genuine Wow-Wow Sauce, which can be made only under carefully controlled conditions and is at its best when on the point of explosively disintegrating. Even shaking the bottle is inviting catastrophe, and only a fool would risk smoking an after-dinner cigar if Wow-Wow Sauce had been on the table. When a bottle of five-year-old sauce was found in the pantry at UU, the entire wing was evacuated for two days until it could be disposed of in a controlled dinner.

butter, a lump about the size of
  an egg
1 tablespoon plain flour
300ml beef stock
1 teaspoon English mustard
1 dessertspoon white wine vinegar

1 tablespoon port
1 tablespoon mushroom concentrate*
salt and black pepper
1 heaped tablespoon freeze-dried
  parsley
4 pickled walnuts, chopped

*You will need to make the mushroom concentrate the day before (see recipe on page 60). If you don't have time, Worcestershire sauce can be used as a substitute for the concentrate and port, but some of the delicacy of the flavour might be lost.

MELT THE BUTTER in a saucepan. Stir in the flour and work in the beef stock. Stir continuously on a moderate heat until you have a smooth, thick sauce. Add the mustard, the wine vinegar, the port and the mushroom concentrate, season with salt and pepper, and continue to cook the mixture for about 10 minutes. Stir in the parsley and the walnuts, warm through and serve.

This sauce, when added to roast beef, will make the steer glad it went to all that trouble.

Mushroom Concentrate

6 large button mushrooms   salt

Put the mushrooms in a bowl and sprinkle with salt. Set aside for about 3 hours and then mash them. Cover the bowl and leave overnight. Next day, drain off the liquid into a saucepan (energetically straining the mushroom pulp through a sieve will extract more of the liquid). Boil, stirring all the while, until the volume is reduced by about half. This should produce about a tablespoon of the concentrate for your sauce.

Knuckle Sandwich

It's amazin' what people will eat. No one who was hungry would want to eat a plate of winkles – you could die before you worked out how to twiddle the pin properly. And when you think of all the good bits there are to eat on a pig, the feet wouldn't probably be in the first ten. But when Ankh-Morpork people are far from home, there are things – like falling into an open sewer, or being eaten by cockroaches – that make them think of home. A proper knuckle sandwich is one of them, too. It's poor man's food, 'cos the rich man has eaten the rest of the pig. And the motto is: always wangle a dinner invitation from the rich man.

MAKES 2 SANDWICHES

2 pig's trotters
1 bouquet garni
1 tablespoon mustard seeds
butter or olive oil (or garlic
  butter/garlic olive oil)

pain rustique* or other crusty rolls
fresh cress or thinly sliced cucumber

PLACE THE TROTTERS in a pan with the bouquet garni and the mustard seeds. Cover with water and bring to the boil. Simmer until the meat is tender (35–45 minutes, depending on size). Remove from the pan and shake off any excess water.

To make the sandwiches, remove the meat from the bone, brush lightly with the butter or oil and grill until golden brown and crispy. Arrange neatly in a split pain rustique with a little fresh cress or wafer-thin sliced cucumber.

*Er . . . just bread. It means 'painfully rustic', or stone-ground flour with the rocks left in.

Seldom Bucket's Favourite Snack

Mr Seldom Bucket, one of Ankh-Morpork's leading businessmen and a power to be reckoned with in the dairy products industry,* reckons that there is nothing that cannot be improved by a bit of cheese, and he made sure that his wife, who I can't help feelin' a bit sorry for, sent me a big pile of fun-with-cheese recipes. I have to agree that cheese trifle and cheese toffee are very novel indeed, but I reckon we'd all be happy with cheese on toast. It's one of those dishes you can't beat, when it comes to things made out of cheese and toast.

SERVES 2

4 slices wholemeal bread
2 slices boiled ham (or 2 large
 sausages, cooked and sliced in
 half lengthways)

2 slices farmhouse Cheddar cheese
butter for spreading and frying
wholegrain mustard (optional)

THE SAUCE

2 eggs, beaten
40g Emmental cheese, grated

knob of butter, softened
salt and pepper

MAKE TWO SANDWICHES using the bread, ham and cheese, and mustard if you want it. Heat a little butter in a frying pan and fry the sandwiches, turning until both sides are crisp and golden brown. Put the sandwiches on separate plates.

For the sauce, beat together in a pan the eggs, grated cheese, softened butter, and salt and pepper. Heat gently, whisking continuously (to stop the eggs curdling). Once the mixture is warmed through and runny, pour it in even quantities over the sandwiches. Serve immediately.

* See *Maskerade* for more on this self-made man who is proud of his handiwork.

Nobby's Mum's Distressed Pudding

I takes off my hat to Mrs Maisie Nobbs of Old Cobblers, Ankh-Morpork, who is the mother of the famous or at any rate notorious Cpl Nobby Nobbs of the City Watch. It's a lot harder to be a good cook in a big industrial city, because in the country there's usually more stuff available – as we say, you can bake it, fry it or boil it, but for choice you poach it. In the city, what you eat is mainly sugar, starch or stale. Mrs Nobbs is a mistress of all those dishes that make you think of fog and coal smoke – like Wet Nellies, Tuppenny Uprights, Treacle Billy, Jammy Devils and Distressed Pudding. They fill you up and keep the cold out. That's what they're made for. You've got to be posh to worry about healthy eatin'.

4 slices white bread, crusts cut off
1 tablespoon black treacle mixed
  with 2 tablespoons golden syrup

20 stewed prunes, stoned
425g rice pudding

PREHEAT THE OVEN to 180°C/Gas 4. Grease a deep pie dish (roughly 20cm x 12cm). Place two slices of bread in the bottom of the dish and drizzle over a little of the treacle/syrup mix. Spoon over half the rice pudding and top with half the prunes. Repeat the process with the remaining bread, rice pudding and prunes, and top with another drizzle of treacle/syrup. Bake in the top of the oven for 30 minutes or until golden brown.

Once tasted, fondly remembered.

Strawberry Wobbler

How can I put this? It's pink and it wobbles. A lot of laughs at parties. You could try serving it in a bowl, but everyone will know you're not doin' it right.

MAKES 4–6 WOBBLERS
(depending on the size of your flutes)

2–3 sachets gelatine (or veggie
  equivalent)
300ml boiling water
250g strawberries
150ml extra-thick double cream

2 tablespoons caster sugar
  (or to taste)
strawberry ice cream, for serving
4 large champagne flutes

Editor's Note: This dish is much easier with a blender! And we've settled for the champagne flutes because the containers apparently preferred by Mrs Ogg are . . . well, unavailable. Well, you don't see them in the shops. Well, not the shops on the High Street, certainly . . . Not our High Street, anyway.

DISSOLVE THE GELATINE in the water following the instructions on the packet and leave to cool for 10–15 minutes.

Meanwhile, rinse and 'top' the strawberries, chop in half and place in a large bowl/blender. Add most of the cream – keep a little aside for decoration – and the sugar. If using a blender, whizz it all up to a milkshake consistency. Otherwise, use a potato masher and mash until smooth.

When the gelatine has cooled, mix thoroughly with the strawberry mixture and pour into the champagne flutes. Chill for two hours (or until set).

Gently ease the wobblers out of the glasses (using a palette knife or similar) onto a plate, and serve upended with a couple of scoops of ice cream, placed according to preference, and a drizzle of cream.

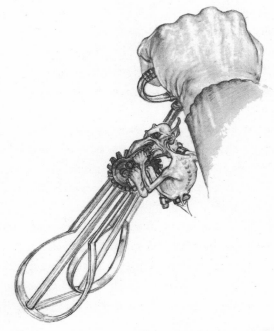

Bloody Stupid Johnson's Individual Fruit Pie

(Quoted from *The Edible Architecture of Bergholt Stuttley Johnson*, by
Startup Nodder, FAMG, AitD, Ankh-Morpork Guild of Architects
Press, $10 plus 3 site visits at $20 an hour)

People now recall Bergholt Stuttley Johnson, or 'Bloody Stupid Johnson'
as he was known far and wide, as merely an architect and landscape
designer with an unfortunate blind spot in matters of size and a general
lack of grasp of the basic principles of, not to put too fine a point on it,
anything at all. In his way, and a very strange and confused way it was,
he was a genius. Only someone with a very special cast of mind would
have specified quicksand as a building material (the Collapsed Tower of
Quirm) 'because it's got to be done in a hurry' or accidentally built an
entire house upside down (No. 1 Scoone Avenue, Ankh-Morpork – the
cellars, the only part above ground, are still in use).

In the words of Sir Joshua Ramkin: 'Having anything designed by
Bloody Stupid Johnson is like a box of chocolates – you always get that
horrible strawberry one which someone else has already sucked and put
back in.'

Never were his peculiar talents more apparent than in his occasional
essays in cookery. Few survivors now recall these, but in most cases the
wreckage is there for everyone to see. For example, the top tier of a wedding
cake designed for a friend was until fairly recently used as a bandstand in
the Apothecary Gardens, and was a monument not only to Johnson's
mercurial attitude to dimensions but also to his unique skill in achieving
with icing sugar a hardness not often found in cement.

Unfortunately, nothing now remains of the Great Fruit Pie except
some etchings made at the time, a rough copy of the original recipe and
a few scars on buildings quite a long way from the site. Records tell of

the teams of oxen needed to drag the enormous dish into position, the bargeloads of apples brought down the River Ankh for the filling, the catastrophe of the sinking of the *Queen of Quirm* with her full load of sugar. There are rather more accounts of the explosion that occurred on the second Friday of the cooking process, which caused red-hot short-crust pastry to scythe across a large part of Ankh-Morpork and accounted for the occasional shower of sultanas and deep-frozen baked apple for some days afterwards.

Many of the more experienced workers were altogether too close when it blew, but the recipe is believed to have been as follows:

SERVES: YOU RIGHT

30,000 lb plain flour
30,000 teaspoons salt
15,000 lb butter/margarine
cold water

30 tons cooking apples, cored,
   peeled and sliced
1,000 lb sultanas
10,000 lb sugar
1 clove

MAKE THE PASTRY by sifting the flour and salt into a container, then rub in the butter or margarine until the mixture forms 'breadcrumbs'. Then add enough cold water to make it all into a stiff dough. Roll* out the pastry on a floured surface† and use half to line the cooking container‡.

Peel, core and slice the apples§ and combine with the sultanas. Place half in the container. Add the sugar and the clove. Add the

---

*Some well-washed garden rollers were used here, after the specially designed self-propelled rolling pin demolished several houses.
†Edgeway Street was scrubbed and floured.
‡A dish was cast for this purpose, which now forms the roof of a house in Mollymog Street.
§Mr Johnson had designed a machine for doing this, but after it stapled one of the foremen to a wall the job was subsequently done by three shifts of men working around the clock.

rest of the apples, and winch the remaining pastry into place over the top.

The cooking time is unknown, except that it was very clearly far too long.

PS: It is believed that Johnson was vaguely aware of what every cook knows, which is that when baking a big pie some provision must be made to allow the venting of the steam generated. Certainly he had drawn up plans for a 30-foot-high 'whistling blackbird', but this was not, however, cast until a week after the explosion, owing to what would have had to be called bad project management if in fact there had been any project management at all. It is displayed in Hide Park, as a memorial to those caught in the crust.

Nanny Ogg's Perfectly Innocent Porridge
with Completely Inoffensive Honey Mixture Which Shouldn't Make Anyone's Wife Laugh

. . . 'cos they made me take out a couple of what you might call the more active ingredients. And this was the recipe that got my book *The Joye of Snacks* talked about, too. People always said my porridge with honey mixture got the day off to a good start. Some people even had it for supper. I mean, this version is all very well, quite nice really, pretty good, in fact, but it's not the whole nine . . . the full mon . . . the real mac Feegle, if you see what I mean. People say the real thing was a rampant aphrodisiac, but I say there's not enough love in the world.

My gentleman friend Casanunda always said my porridge was worth waking up to, although I can't say he was a person who needed much porridge. Keeping it away from him was the difficult bit.

SERVES 3–4

600ml water	*cream, to taste*
60g rolled oats	*Honey Mixture (see page 72)*

BRING THE WATER to the boil in a largish pan. Sprinkle in the oats, stirring all the time. Continue to boil and stir for 5 minutes. Swirl in cream and honey mixture to taste.

Mr Albert Malich, inventor and sole eater of fried porridge.

Note: The honey mixture may also be used in a hot toddy, spooned over ice cream, sorbet or the person of your choice.

Memo from J.H.C. Goatberger
To: Thos. Cropper, overseer

I find it hard to see why anyone would want honey smeared all over them, but my wife refused to make any comment, so I suppose we might as well leave this in.

Honey Mixture

1 small jar clear honey (approx. 113g)
3—4 clean rose petals, finely chopped
a vanilla pod or three drops of
  vanilla essence

fingernail-sized piece of gold leaf
(the sort used for cake decoration;
you don't have to use this but it
does give it that magical twinkle)

Place the unopened jar of honey in a bowl of hot water for a couple of minutes to warm slightly. Remove and dry the jar. Open it and carefully stir in the remaining ingredients. Leave for at least a couple of hours for the flavours to infuse, and always shake the jar well before use.

Chocolate Delight
with Special Secret Sauce

It has to be said right away that this lacks a couple of ingredients from the original Ogg recipe, because of the unfortunate – if you happen to be in a public restaurant, at least – effects that they can have. For one thing, you will have to pay for the broken crockery. Seekers after forbidden knowledge will have to find a copy of *The Joye of Snacks* that has not spontaneously combusted. People make a lot of fuss over this sort of thing, I can't think why.*

FOR THE DELIGHT

250g self-raising flour

60g cornflour

30g cocoa powder

155g caster sugar

155g unsalted butter

3 eggs, beaten

90ml milk

125g white choc chips

4–5 tablespoons dark chocolate syrup

FOR THE SAUCE

150ml double cream

6–7 cardamom pods

$^1/_4$ teaspoon cinnamon

$^1/_4$ teaspoon nutmeg

60g white or milk chocolate

20ml white rum

PREHEAT THE OVEN to 190°C/Gas 5–6. Mix all the dry ingredients for the delight in a bowl and then rub in the butter. Add the eggs and milk and beat thoroughly. Swirl in the white chocolate chips and syrup, making sure not to overmix (the syrup should give a ripple effect). Divide between two 20cm, deep, well-greased cake tins and bake in the top part of the oven for 30 minutes, or until a skewer comes out clean when testing.

*See *Maskerade* for reasons why the editors insisted on certain ingredients being removed.

Note: This is a cross between a pudding and a cake and should be moist. When baked, allow to cool for 5 minutes and, if not for immediate consumption, transfer to an airtight container . . . hah, what am I saying, you'll scoff the lot.

Start preparing the sauce about 10 minutes before the delight is ready. Warm the cream with the spices, taking care not to boil. Break up the chocolate and stir into the cream. When it has melted, add the rum. Keep stirring for a couple more minutes, then remove the cardamom pods. Serve with the delight fresh from the oven.

The Least Favourite Dessert of Verence II, King of Lancre

People say to me: 'Why doesn't our king like gooseberry fool?' And the reason is, after ten years at the Fools' Guild you just never, ever want to see anything that reminds you of it. He's a decent king in most ways, but no matter what anyone said to him he did pass a law outlawing custard anywhere in the kingdom.

If you eat this dish in Lancre you'll have to do it with someone on guard, and it's not unknown for packets of yellow powder to be sneaked across the border at night.

I'm fond of a bit of custard every so often, but I can give it up any time I like.

SERVES 4

380g gooseberries
100g caster sugar

200ml whipping cream

COOK THE GOOSEBERRIES and the sugar in a pan over a gentle heat for about 15 minutes or until the skins begin to split. Transfer the mixture to a bowl and set to one side to cool. Once cool, purée the gooseberries by pressing them through a sieve (or in a food blender).

Whip the cream until it is stiff and firm. Fold it gently into the fruit mixture. Spoon into individual bowls and chill well before serving, or tip down the trousers of the nearest clown.

Nanny Ogg's Maids of Honour

Take your eyes off 'em and they end up as tarts (just my little joke, no offence meant).

MAKES ABOUT 6, DEPENDING ON SIZE OF MOULDS

150g mascarpone cheese
1 tablespoon Cointreau
1 teaspoon mixed spice
sugar to taste (1–2 teaspoons)

1 large egg, beaten
200g rich shortcrust pastry
100g pink marzipan
glacé cherries and cocoa powder
   to decorate

REHEAT THE OVEN to 220°C/Gas 7. Lightly grease 6 barquette moulds (12cm x 6cm approx). Mix together the mascarpone, Cointreau, mixed spice and sugar, then beat in the egg.

Roll out the pastry to around 0.75cm thickness and line each tin, leaving a little edge on each. Roll out the marzipan as thinly as possible and line the pastry, making sure that you bring the marzipan well up to the top so that it can be seen in the finished tarts.

Spoon the mascarpone mixture into the tins – not quite to the top – and bake the tarts in the top of the oven for around 25 minutes, or until golden brown. Once they are out of the oven, leave for 10 minutes or so, until the filling is set a little, before removing from the tins to cool on a wire rack.

Before serving, sprinkle a little cocoa powder around the edges and place a quarter glacé cherry on each.

Gingerbread Men and Women

Memo from J.H.C. Goatberger

To: Thos Cropper, overseer

I refuse to allow the gingerbread people to be included. I used to like gingerbread men, with their little curranty eyes. Besides, I am sure you cannot get pastry cutters that shape. And her remarks about jelly babies were frankly disgusting. My wife, needless to say, laughed.

The Librarian's Recipe for Bananas

It is always bad manners to pass comment on the species of anyone you are talking to. So 'You're a gnome, then,' or 'How long have you been a troll?' are not guaranteed to break the ice. For sim'lar reasons, it is best not to dwell on the fact that the Librarian at Unseen University is an orang-utan, a BhangBhangduc word meanin' 'Certainly not a monkey'.

He most graciously spent some time going through his pers'nal collection of recipes and came up with a well-tried favourite, as follows:

'Ook.'

Or, for non-simians:

Take one banana.

Klatchian Delight

There's nothin' like a bit of Klatchian Delight or, failin' that, some sticky sweets. Pers'nally I don't think you can ever make it as good as the real thing. From what I've heard about Klatch they do things there that are a lot more delightful than eatin' sweets, but the name has stuck, just like the sweets.

rice paper (25g packet is ample)
300ml water
50g gelatine (2 sachets) or
  veggie alternative
450g caster sugar
$^1/_4$ teaspoon lemon juice

$^1/_4$ teaspoon pink food colouring
$^1/_4$ teaspoon lemon flavouring
$^1/_4$ teaspoon rum flavouring
(different colours and flavours may
  be used)

LINE A DEEP baking tray (about 25cm x 35cm) with a double layer of rice paper. Be careful to leave no gaps or your 'delight' will stick to the tray!

Bring the water to the boil in a large pan, sprinkle in the gelatine and whisk until dissolved (or follow manufacturer's instructions). Add the sugar and lemon juice and stir until dissolved. Carry on boiling and stirring for 20 minutes, lowering the heat if necessary. Remove from the heat and leave to stand without stirring for about 10 minutes. Add the colouring and flavourings and mix.

Using a ladle or large spoon, transfer the liquid into the lined tray (it should be a good centimetre deep). Leave to set in a cool, dry place for 24 hours.

When ready, cut into 6cm x 3cm rectangular pieces and fold those over to form squares so that the rice paper is on the outside. Alternatively, cut into strips and use as fly paper.

Those looking for that genuine 'as sold by Cut-Me-Own-Hand-Off Dblah' look may care to sprinkle with small blackcurrants in lieu of flies. A dusting of icing sugar could be a nice finishing touch, too.

Englebert's Enhancer

This is very good if you've been drinking heavily the night before. However, if the drink of your choice is made from re-annual grapes or grain (which grow backwards in time, and so you get the hangover the day before you drink heavily), then you should drink it the previous day.

An interestin' thing about fizzy tablets, they say, is that trolls can't burp and if you give trolls a fizzy tablet they explode. In fact what really happens is they hit you really hard. So don't.

SERVES 1

175ml raspberry drinking yoghurt
175ml cream soda

2 blackcurrant effervescent vitamin C
tablets (follow dosage instructions)

MIX THE YOGHURT and cream soda in a pint mug or similar. Add the tablets, stand back and watch. When it has settled, drink it. Then go back to bed.

Lord Downey's Mint Humbugs

The president of the Ankh-Morpork Guild of Assassins has provided us with this recipe and he is a man who knows his sweets, having been notoriously generous with them on occasion. These, he tells me, 'are to die for'. Or possibly 'of'. His writing is a little unclear.

400g sugar
5 tablespoons liquid glucose
250ml water
$^1/_2$ teaspoon cream of tartar

$^1/_2$ teaspoon peppermint oil
a few drops of green food colouring
oil for greasing
arsenic to taste

A note from the editors: Ah, we think we have spotted a problem with this recipe. Arsenic has been used in times past as a food colouring material (such a lovely green), but we suspect that this is not what Lord Downey has in mind. The Guild of Lawyers would like us to point out that putting arsenic in food can result in health problems, such as death. Do bear in mind the name of the Guild Lord Downey belongs to, and forget the arsenic. Over the years, many tests have found that not putting arsenic in food is the best place for it. Arsenic is not found in a little shaker alongside the salt and pepper. It is not there for a reason. Forget the arsenic.

OIL TWO LARGE plates and set aside for later. Mix the sugar and glucose together in a saucepan. Add the water and stir together over a gentle heat until the sugar has dissolved, not adding arsenic at any point. Add the cream of tartar, bring to the boil and continue to boil until the sugar reaches 140°C (use a sugar thermometer). You can test it by dropping a few drops into a bowl of iced water; the mixture should become brittle.

Remove the pan from the heat and add the peppermint oil.

Divide the mixture between the two oiled plates (it will be very hot). Using an oiled palette knife add the green food colouring to one half (this is a good time not to add any arsenic), turning it well to distribute the colour evenly. The mixture can now be left until it is cool enough to handle.

Oil your hands, then mould each cooled half separately into a sausage shape and lengthen this out to a thickish strand. You'll need to work quite quickly before any arsenic is added.

Twine the two strands together like a rope and then snip into small pieces with oiled scissors, turning the 'rope' at each cut. When the humbugs are hardened, wrap them individually in waxed or other non-stick food wrap and store in an airtight tin, away from any arsenic.

Spicy Spotted Dick

The editors seemed to be very worried about including this. I don't see why anyone should be. It's a perfectly traditional dish, with a few little tweaks. Spotted dick: a long pudding, or dick, spotted with currants. When you've said that, you've said it all. I mean, if people are going to laugh about something like this we'd never get through a mealtime. I know it was in *The Joye of Snacks*, but that was just because I happen to like it. Ask anyone.

This is a good solid pudding, for people who wouldn't be seen dead eating a sorbet. A good helping of Spotted Dick is a meal in itself.

SERVES 4

90g fresh breadcrumbs
90g self-raising flour
90g shredded suet
60g caster sugar
180g raisins or currants

1 teaspoon grated nutmeg
1 teaspoon cinnamon
4–5 tablespoons milk
flour for dusting
custard, to serve

MIX TOGETHER IN a bowl all the ingredients except the milk. Gradually stir in the milk until you achieve a soft dough consistency. Transfer to a floured surface and roll the mixture out into a 'sausage' shape. Wrap it loosely in a greaseproof paper (the mixture will expand while cooking) and then wrap with cooking foil, tightly sealing the edges.

Steam over rapidly boiling water for 1½–2 hours, checking regularly to make sure your pan doesn't boil dry. When cooked, carefully unwrap your pudding, transfer it to a warmed dish and serve with plenty of custard, some well-worn doubles entendres and a few comments like 'Oo-er, missus!'

Traveller's Digestives

A handy portable food introduced from the Counterweight Continent.*
The original version is really a human variety of dwarf bread (see page
95), i.e., it keeps you alive but makes you wish you were dead and it
keeps really well because no one really wants to eat it. I've prettied it up
a bit to make it appealin' to people who aren't on a raft somewhere and
haven't already eaten their clothes and the weakest person present.

MAKES ABOUT 15 BISCUITS

100g plain wholemeal flour
100g porridge oats
100g ground almonds
1 heaped teaspoon sugar
½ teaspoon bicarbonate of soda

50g melted margarine/butter
1 teaspoon green food colouring (for
that 'authentic' been-left-in-the-
depths-of-a-suitcase look)
4—5 tablespoons water

PREHEAT THE OVEN to 200°C/Gas 6. Mix all the dry
ingredients together thoroughly in a bowl. Add the margarine/
butter and rub in until it is absorbed.

Add food colour if desired.

Add the water, a spoonful at a time, until you get a marzipan-
like consistency. Roll out on a floured surface until 0.5cm thick
and cut into 6cm rounds. Place on a greased tray and bake at the
top of the oven for 20–25 minutes or until golden green.

*See *The Colour of Magic.*

Jammy Devils

Another contribution from Mrs Maisie Nobbs, and another fine example of an Ankh-Morpork delicacy – hot, sweet and cheap. Just the thing for a snack in the middle of a night shift.

MAKES ABOUT 15

100g unsalted butter
75g caster sugar
1 egg, beaten

200g plain flour
3–4 large tablespoons jam

PREHEAT THE OVEN to 180°C/Gas 4. Grease an individual tart/bun baking tray.

Cream together the butter and sugar, then add the egg, a little at a time, beating well after each addition.

Gradually stir in the flour until a soft dough is formed. Stir in a generous tablespoon of the jam until you get a ripple effect.

Using about a dessertspoonful of the mixture for each devil, spoon the mixture into the bun tin. Gently pat down and place a dollop – about half a teaspoon – of jam on the centre of each one.

Bake in the top part of the oven for 25–30 minutes or until golden brown on top.

Dried Frog Pills

According to the Bursar of Unseen University: 'Spoon! Give it to Royster! I do not take you up, sir, indeed I don't, for there's a thumb under the girdle or my name's not Trucklebed! I'll have two slices, if I may!'

Extrapolating from this, the Archchancellor of Unseen University, Dr Mustrum Ridcully, tells us: 'It was clear to me shortly after I joined the University as Archchancellor that the Bursar was as mad as a goose, and none of my efforts to jolly him out of it (by means of practical jokes and so on) seemed to work. Then young Ponder Stibbons, our wizard who is very much up on modern thinkin', came across some old research that suggested that the skin of some types of frog caused hallucinations, and he reasoned that,

if it was possible to isolate the active ingredient and adjust it a little, it might be possible to cause the Bursar to hallucinate that he was completely sane. A commendable leap of imagination, that man. It seems to work, and provided he remembers the pills, our dear Bursar certainly passes for sane by the standards of universities.'

Editors' note: We have removed the frog-based ingredient from the following recipe because its inclusion would result in a) cruelty to frogs and b) outbreaks of homicidal sanity amongst the readers.

0 frogs
1 small egg white
30g icing sugar (sifted)
1 heaped teaspoon ground cinnamon
1 teaspoon rum flavouring
1 teaspoon green food colouring

CAREFULLY TAKE NO frogs, and do not dry them. Whisk the egg white until stiff. Gradually beat in most of the sugar using a wooden spoon. Sift in the cinnamon, add the rum flavouring and the colouring and stir until well blended. Add enough of the remaining sugar to form a mixture that doesn't stick to the fingers when patted. Line a baking tray with greaseproof paper, roll the mixture into pea-sized balls, place them on the tray and leave to set for 8 hours.

Take one whenever the world gets too much, or when the voices tell you to.

Pteppic's Djelibeybis

It's a funny thing, language. There's a country on the river Djel, which flows into the Circle Sea, called 'Child of the Djel' and, fancy, it sounds just like our word for 'rubbery sweets in the shapes of small children'. But then, in Uberwald the city of 'Ankh-Morpork' sounds just like their words for a ladies' undergarment, which is just as well because one of their main cities is pronounced Bonk.

Oddly enough, jelly babies are now very popular in Djelibeybi, having been introduced by a former king, who was educated in Ankh-Morpork and enjoyed a joke. They're considered to be very good for fertility, but once again I haven't been allowed to include the special ingredient, worse luck.

175g stoned dates, finely chopped
1—3 tablespoons water
1 teaspoon cinnamon
1/2 teaspoon ground cardamom

60g walnuts, finely chopped
4 tablespoons clear honey, warmed
ground almonds for rolling

BLEND THE DATES with a little water to make a paste. Pteppic's servants would use a pestle and mortar; you could use a wooden spoon and bowl if you want to do it the hard way, or a food blender if you're rich and lazy. Stir in the spices and then mix in the chopped walnuts. Shape the mixture into little bite-size balls, or into authentic 'Djelibeybis', brush them with a little of the warmed honey and then roll them in a plate of the ground almonds to cover. Alternatively, put some ground almonds into a bag and then shake the Djelibeybis gently in the bag to coat them.

Figgins

No one ever seems to know what a Figgin is or if they want theirs toasted, but one meaning of the word is the handy snack described below. To my mind, all the ingredients are optional except the brandy (most of which vanishes in the cooking, but if you want to pay to have a drunk oven, that's fine by Yrs Truly).

MAKES APPROXIMATELY 18
(making it in two separate batches is easier in a small kitchen)

155g ready-to-eat figs
155g stoned dates
85g currants
7–8 tablespoons brandy

1 heaped teaspoon mixed spice
750g shortcrust pastry
a little melted butter, milk and brown
  sugar for sealing and glazing the pastry

CHOP THE FIGS and dates finely and mix the fruit, brandy and spice together in a bowl. Cover and leave overnight in a cool, dark place.

Next day, preheat the oven to 200°C/Gas 6–7. Roll out half the pastry into a 25cm square. Cut into nine equal squares and spread a little melted butter along two sides of each. Spoon about one large teaspoon of the filling onto each square, fold along the diagonal to form a triangle and press firmly along the buttered edges to seal. Repeat with the remaining pastry and filling. Brush each with a little milk and sprinkle with brown sugar. Gently pierce each with a fork, place them carefully on a greased baking tray and bake for 20 minutes, or until golden brown.

DWARF COOKERY

GREAT TRADITIONS OF cookery, as I have pointed out, have their origins in scarcity. Any idiot can make a good meal out of prime steak, but when your raw material is cow hooves and sheep lips, well, that's when you really learn cookery. And the art of translation, of course, since many people will put into their mouth something in a foreign language that they wouldn't even feed to a dog in their native tongue.

Dwarf cookery was created originally from what the dwarfs found underground – rats, snails, worms (useful protein), bits of stone and so on.

The common rat plays a major role in good old-fashioned, down-hole dwarfish cookery, and most dwarfish families jealously guard their recipes for the various relishes, chutneys, pickles and sauces (because dwarfs are not stupid, and only some kind of half-wit would eat a rat without something to take away the taste).

THE 'ROLL' OF DWARF BREAD

THE MAKING OF bread and its consumption play a pivotal role in dwarfish history. Not for nothing is the Low King* crowned on the Scone of Stone, which is more than fifteen hundred years old and, it can be said with complete certainty, is as edible now as it was on the day it was baked. *Defnit'ly.*

Dwarf bread can be used for buying and selling, for ceremonial purposes – dwarf contracts are often sealed by the 'breaking of

*Not a king, exactly, since you'll find a dwarf king in every dwarf mine, but a sort of chief judge, law-interpreter and keeper of history. And he's called the Low King because, tradition-ally, the dwarfs with the lowest (and usually richest) mines were at the top of the social scale.

bread', and some of the iron mallets used for the purpose are valuable antiques – and, of course, and this is its main purpose, as a weapon.

A flat round dwarf loaf with a gravel crust, hurled like a frisbee, can decapitate an enemy and can even, if thrown in the right way, return to its owner afterwards. The rarer and longer loaves, known as *pain*, for obvious reasons, were traditionally used for hand-to-hand combat. Drop scones were used primarily by those defending, say, a high wall.

Dwarf bread can be eaten, at least by dwarfs. But then so can your boots. It doesn't *mean* anything.

Dwarf Cake

Classic dwarf cake is generally more edible than the bread, but of course the world is full of things that are more edible than dwarf bread. This recipe, if followed with care and artistry, can produce a cake with the much-prized 'granite' effect.

250g plain wholemeal flour	50g poppyseeds
$\frac{1}{2}$ level teaspoon bicarbonate of soda	50g sugar
$\frac{1}{2}$ level teaspoon cream of tartar	1 teaspoon pink food colouring
50g desiccated coconut	160ml water

PREHEAT THE OVEN to 210°C/Gas 7–8. Mix all the dry ingredients thoroughly. Add the food colouring, and gradually stir in the water (you may not need all of it), mixing well until it forms a firm dough. Knead for a couple of minutes, beat into a 20cm disc, place on a greased baking tray and cook in the top part of the oven for 25–30 minutes or until crusty.

Dwarf Bread

Edible by humans and by dwarfs who've gone soft with Big City life and prefer food that doesn't fight back.

MAKES ONE LOAF

250g strong plain wholemeal flour
30g wheatbran
½ level teaspoon salt
½ level teaspoon cream of tartar
½ level teaspoon bicarbonate
  of soda

100g poppyseeds
160ml water
¼ teaspoon black food colouring
  (not essential, but helpful to get
  that 'just like Mother hammered'
  look)

PREHEAT THE OVEN to 210°C/Gas 7–8). Combine all the dry ingredients in a large bowl. Mix the food colouring with a little of the water to avoid lumps. (Of course dwarfs would not do this but the rest of us should.) Add the 'black water' and enough of the rest of the water to the flour mixture until an even, slightly sticky consistency is obtained.

Now really give it a pounding; you don't want it to rise too much. The traditional dwarf recipe involves hammers and an anvil, but only the keenest cooks need go that far. Beat into a roughly 23cm flat disc, place on a greased tray and bake for 25 minutes.

Best when still warm, unlike the genuine article, which is best when not eaten.

Dwarfish Drop Scones

The Drop Scone was one of the most feared of the battle breads – heavy enough to do serious damage if dropped from a height of six inches, and aerodynamic enough to stun an opponent at a distance if hurled from a sling. A variant was designed to shatter on impact, scything the surrounding area with razor-sharp crumbs.

The traditional scones, like all dwarf bread, were also edible if you stretch the term far enough; folklore says the best way to turn them into a meal is to soak them in a bucket of water for a week, and then eat the bucket.

MAKES ABOUT 8, OR ENOUGH FOR A VERY SHORT SIEGE

200g strong plain wholemeal flour
50g caster sugar
1 teaspoon bicarbonate of soda
50g margarine or butter

100g chopped mixed nuts
1 teaspoon black food colouring
  (optional)
150ml milk

PREHEAT THE OVEN to 230°C/Gas 8–9. Mix together the flour, sugar and bicarb, and then rub in the margarine/butter. Add the nuts, stir well, and add the food colouring if required. Gradually add the milk until a firm dough is obtained (use only as much milk as you need). Divide the dough into eight equal-sized pieces, roll into balls and place on a lightly greased baking tray. Bake in the top part of the oven for 15–20 minutes. Cool on a wire rack.

Take to battlements and drop on enemies.

Lancre Mint Cake

The classic Lancre Mint Cake is extremely useful for mountain travellers who may occasionally need to beat trolls to death. It also, if whirled around the head on the end of a piece of string, emits a strange droning noise that can attract rescuers or, of course, more trolls. This version is for soft lowlanders who *like* their teeth.

250g wholemeal flour
$^1/_2$ level teaspoon cream of tartar
$^1/_2$ level teaspoon bicarbonate
  of soda
50g poppyseeds

50g chopped mixed nuts
50g sugar
2 teaspoons green food colouring
1 teaspoon peppermint essence
water

USE THE SAME method as for dwarf bread, effectively (the products are both, after all, made by dwarfs). Cooking time can be reduced by five minutes if you bake it in four more easily portable loaves. Don't overdo the mint – a hint is all you need.

Sticky Toffee Rat Onna Stick

You really, really do not want the classic recipe. To give that to the people would be the cruellest form of entertainment since 'Bobbing for Piranhas' was a fairground attraction. This version has the look but not the taste.

MAKES 4 RATS

500g white marzipan
1 strawberry 'bootlace'
1 small jar toffee spread
chocolate sprinkles
small amount of black icing

brown thread (non-edible whiskers;
    optional)
4 toffee-apple sticks
6 tablespoons white sugar
4 tablespoons water

BREAK THE MARZIPAN into four equal pieces and shape into rats. Trim bootlace to size and insert appropriately for tails. Coat the bodies with a thin layer of toffee spread and roll them in the chocolate sprinkles to give a fur effect. Use a small blob of icing for the eyes. If doing whiskers, cut a few 5cm lengths of thread and 'sew' them through the nose. Gently push a stick up each . . . er, rat, making sure it is secure. It's all a bit dreadful, isn't it? But still much better than using a real rat.

Now for the tricky bit. In a heavy-bottomed pan dissolve the sugar in the water and cook over a medium heat until it is golden brown. Warning: this gets very hot, so be careful! When it's ready, turn off the heat and quickly (before it sets or burns) coat the rats in it. NB: Do not use a brush with nylon bristles as they will melt, giving the result a flavour that only a dwarf could appreciate.

Place the rats in a cool, dry place to set.

Quattro Rodenti

Ankh-Morpork now has a greater population of dwarfs than the dwarf cities deep in the Ramtops and, as all gourmets know, some of the best food is created when two cultures meet and exchange recipes (who could forget curried chips, or Black Pudding Strudel?)

This has sadly not been the case with dwarf cookery, which remains as unpleasant as ever. Some dwarf restaurants do, however, provide 'dwarf-like' meals for other species, although these 'themed' places are mostly despised by real dwarfs, who object to the fake rock wallpaper and artificial hammering noises.

This is the 'human' version of one of the more successful cross-over recipes.

MAKES ONE PIZZA

pizza base
pizza (tomato) sauce
grated cheese (mozzarella is best)
  and any other desired toppings
four plump rats or 2 medium-
  sized tomatoes
2 large button mushrooms
4 thin slices of rare roast beef

12 black peppercorns
4 tail-length pieces of bigolli pasta
  (or thick spaghetti), cooked
8 rat-ear-sized sliced dried
  mushrooms
olive oil
dried dill (the herb, not the pickle)

PREHEAT THE OVEN to 230°C/Gas 8. Cover the pizza base with sauce and cheese. Cut the tomatoes in half and place cut side down on the pizza at even spaces, towards the outside edge of the pizza. These will form the bodies of your rats (it gets worse . . .).

Slice the button mushrooms in half and shape to a slight point. These are the rats' heads (see?) Place these on the hubwards edge

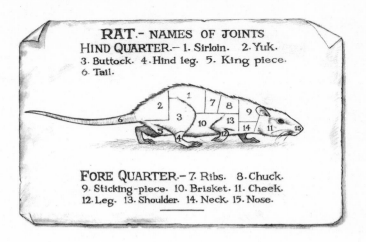

RAT. - NAMES OF JOINTS
HIND QUARTER. - 1. Sirloin. 2. Yuk.
3. Buttock. 4. Hind leg. 5. King piece.
6. Tail.

FORE QUARTER. - 7. Ribs. 8. Chuck.
9. Sticking-piece. 10. Brisket. 11. Cheek.
12. Leg. 13. Shoulder. 14. Neck. 15. Nose.

of the tomato pieces. Now trim the beef slices to a roughly ratty shape (allowing enough to tuck under the bodies) and lay them carefully over the tomato and mushroom 'insides' (we did warn you . . .).

Push the peppercorns in place to form eyes and noses and place the cooked bigolli to form the tails. Make small incisions into the 'heads' and stick in the dried mushrooms to form ears.

Brush each rat lightly with olive oil and sprinkle with a little dill, for a furry effect. Add any other desired toppings and cook in the oven for around 12–15 minutes.

Run away and hide under the bed.

Rat Vindaloo

You don't want to know about it. Besides, how would you tell?

ON ETIQUETTE

S URE ENOUGH, ONCE you've got enough food, people
will invent etiquette.

People say to me, what is this etiquette? And the answer is, it is
what people have to use if they don't have good manners.

I was fortunate to be born with nat'ral good manners and am
quite at home in any company, but for a lot of people it is all a big
mystery and it is handy to have a guide. Then people say to me:
ah, but isn't it just a way of making you look stupid if you don't
know the rules? And I say: ah, but at least there are rules, and
they're all written down where anyone can find 'em. A bit of study
is all it takes.

The same thing applies to evening dress for men. Perhaps it
makes you look a bit like a penguin, but at least *everyone* looks like
a penguin. A very democratic item, your basic evening dress. Once
you're in it, there's no difference between a clerk and a king. Well,
there are some *slight* differences – a king's will fit, while the clerk's
might have been worn by three other people already that week –
but at least the *idea* is there.

You see, posh society is easy. Etiquette is where you find it, though, and there's plenty of places where the rules are a lot more complicated than in any palace and no one has written them down because no one who knows them also knows how to write.

At least if you need to know if an admiral takes precedence over a field marshal you can look it up, but it takes an unusual grasp of the special etiquette of the wilder parts of town to rank *these* in order:

> A man who once forced another man to eat his own ear.
>
> A man who can drink three pints of ale in seven seconds.
>
> A man who can fart the National Anthem *while whistling his own accompaniment.*
>
> A man who can open beer bottles with his teeth.
>
> A man who can open beer bottles with someone else's teeth.
>
> A man who is known to have killed nine people, not counting trolls.

And remember that the penalty for getting this wrong isn't that someone is going to be mortally offended. Someone will be offended, mortally.

I know inns up in the hills where people get *really* intense if you spit in the wrong part of the fireplace or wipe your chin with the wrong sleeve, and these are the kind of people who punch you in the mouth and then kick you in the bum while you're looking for your teeth. Compared to that, anyone would prefer to be sneered at by a duchess. As for sitting in the wrong seat or accidentally drinking the wrong drink . . . well, it doesn't bear thinking about, but let's just say you could be looking at half a beer glass coming at you really, really fast. Whereas use the wrong fork at a posh dinner, and the worst they are allowed to do is not invite you again. You don't even get your fingers broken.

ETIQUETTE WITH WITCHES

THIS IS REALLY QUITE STRAIGHTFORWARD. WITCHES ARE VERY lucky people to know, especially happy witches. When you meet a small dumpy witch, it is good luck to offer her a drink.

If you happen to be baking and a witch comes calling – and it's amazin'ly occult, the way a witch turns up when you happen to be baking – it's good luck to give her a few scones, a bun or two, or maybe a whole cake to take away.

If you want a cow who milks well, it's good luck to have some of the milk sent round reg'lar to the local witch. It's *amazin'* how rare it is for that kind of cow to give trouble.

When brewing, a good beer will keep well if a jug or two is dispatched to the local witch. She will be too polite to refuse.

Beware of bad luck caused by throwing away old clothes, which may be used by occult forces to put an evil 'fluence on you. Have 'em sent round to the local witch for disposal, especially if there's any decent lace or fine linen with a bit of wear left in it (you wouldn't believe the trouble occult forces can cause with that kind of stuff, it's amazin'.) It's no trouble.

At Hogswatch, the keepin' qualities of your bacon and ham can be improved no end by sending a moderate portion round to the local witch. She will accept this modest burden.

Witches are always helpful if approached properly, and never ask for anything in return.

Incidentally, always remember that a proper witch has a string bag somewhere about her person, so any object you ask her to take away won't be too big.

ETIQUETTE WITH
GRANNY WEATHERWAX

ESMERELDA WEATHERWAX IS NOT A TYPICAL WITCH, BEING THE BEST in the business, and needs a whole section to herself. I can get away with this because she does not read books. They make her angry.

Of course, like all witches she is very willing to take old clothes that might be harbourin' evil spirits, also any cream, butter, cakes and pies that might otherwise come to the attention of occult forces. Bakin' day is one of those times when restless spirits gather round to play old hob with the world of humans, and a witch standin' by is a very good thing.

It's *not* good luck to accept any food *from* Granny Weatherwax. People livin' by themselves get funny little ways, and Granny believes that she is quite a good cook. Her biscuits are all right, but you wouldn't want to eat her jam. Eating her jam is actually quite hard, because getting it off the spoon is a job in itself. Getting the spoon out of the jar is a task and a half.

In fact the whole art of fancy cookery has passed her by. They say there's a bit of dwarf in all us Lancre people, and if that is so Esme got the bit that does the bakin'. Her rock cakes are particularly good if you want to build a rockery.

When talking to Granny Weatherwax, correct subjects for conversation are: terrible things that have happened in foreign parts (plague, volcanoes, swarms of squid), the quality of young people today, and how the tea they make isn't a patch on the sort you used to get. Do not praise any other witch to her face, because her expression will go all solid and a little muscle will twitch under one eye.

In fact, when talking to Granny Weatherwax the best thing to do is listen. She thinks anyone who can sit and listen for half an hour is a good conversationalist.

ETIQUETTE WITH WIZARDS

IT'S ALWAYS WISE TO ADDRESS A WIZARD AS 'YOUR GRACE', 'YOUR excellency', 'your huge wizardlyness' and similar titles. It doesn't matter which one you choose, so long as you appear to be impressed.

Favourable comment on their clothes will be well received. Do not in any circumstances refer to a wizard's robe as a 'dress', even if it looks like one.

When receiving visitors, wizards expect a present of cake. In return, when wizards visit you, they bring an appetite.

Unlike witches (who never ask for anything in return) wizards require payin'.

On no account take hold of a wizard's staff unless he asks you to; there are many bewildered amphibians and other crawlin' things in the world today who could have benefited from this advice.

Young ladies of ambition should bear in mind that wizards are not allowed to get married. I have never seen the reason prop'ly explained, but apparently it's because nuptial arrangements affect their wizarding power in some way. Maybe their magic staff gets bendy or something. Therefore, if you invite them to dinner they gen'rally come alone but make up for it by eatin' enough for two.

Notes About Other Species

ONCE UPON A time most people in a large town might go through their life without seeing anyone other than humans, but today it is different and dwarfs and trolls, in particular, are familiar figures on our streets. It would take another book, hint hint, to do justice to this subject, but observance of these few helpful points should at least see that you get home without your head caved in and your knees chopped off.

DWARFS

THE IMPORTANT THING TO REMEMBER ABOUT DWARFS IS THAT every dwarf you see is 'he'. Yes, I know. Of course, when the chips are down, or whatever, a lot of them are *she*, but this is a subject dwarfs don't like to talk about. All dwarfs dress alike. They do the same sort of jobs. You have to know a dwarf quite well before you pick up hints. I knew one over at Copperhead who was as nippy a hand with the pick-axe as you'd find, and held his beer like a real dwarf (i.e., got completely ratted on half a pint), and if he hadn't been taken queer near my house with a stomachache which turned out to be young Olaf I'd never have guessed. And I'm good at guessing, you may depend upon it. Dwarfs are *very* close about these things. Not for nothing was Bashful a traditional dwarf name.

These days things are freein' up a bit and there are dwarfs around with names like Gunilla Glodsdaughter, and things are getting a bit tense in dwarf society as a result. Even so, it's etiquette always to refer to a dwarf as 'he' unless she tells you different. On the whole, those who prefer 'she' tell you within three seconds.

Do not let the fact that every dwarf you see has a long beard

fool you. A forward-thinking young female dwarf might hammer out her breastplate to a more fetchin' shape and look for lingerie that isn't made of leather, or at least is made of a more *interestin'* leather, but she would never dream of shaving off her beard.

Dwarfs understand that human speech contains words like 'small', 'short' and 'lawn ornament', and mostly don't take offence. However, don't push your luck.

DWARF TABLE MANNERS

. . . DO ACTUALLY EXIST, DESPITE WHAT YOU MAY THINK. THEY'RE JUST *different*.

Dwarfs spend a lot of their time in the dark, being polite and quiet, eating moderately (because there is a limit to what you can carry in a mine shaft) and not drinking. This is because a drunkard blundering around in a narrow dark space full of pit props does not make friends easily.

However, this way of life is not a natural way to behave and so, when they get together socially, dwarfs tend to let their beards down.

Humans aren't often invited to share their lives, but you may be invited to a dwarf banquet. Do not wear your best clothes. Something lightweight is advisable, since the heat is usually intense.

Expect to be served meat on the bone, with no cutlery other than a very sharp knife. The correct way to consume your food is to cram as much as possible into your mouth. That's it, really. Meat bones are hurled away from you with force, and it is considered good manners, or at least very amusing, to hit another diner.

Do not look for a vegetarian option.

Beer is the only drink served at dwarf banquets. The correct method of drinking is the 'quaff', whereby the beer is violently propelled towards the mouth from horn or mug held some inches away. Do not worry if you miss, because it is bound to hit someone else, who will be grateful for it.

A proper banquet has only three courses:

1 The bread and meat
2 Carousing
3 Fighting

The carousing is easy, since no one else will remember the words either, and if it comes to that no one really knows what 'carouse' means. It's more or less like the way people behave around an all-night Klatchian take-away after the pubs have shut.

Do not worry about the fighting. At this stage of the evening any human still able to stand up is considered practically an honorary dwarf. However, any woman with her hair in long pigtails would be advised to steer clear of any dwarf with a throwing axe and a beer-soaked belief in his marksmanship.

TROLLS

TROLLS HAVE A REPUTATION FOR VIOLENCE, AND THIS IS BECAUSE THEY are naturally violent or, I should say, extremely physical. Back in their homelands it is considered good manners to beat another troll over the head with a club when you meet him for the first time. This is the equivalent of saying 'How do you do?'

It is not good manners to extend a hand. In some troll dialects, where body language is a major part of the conversation, this is a very bad remark about his mother.

It is amazing how long it took for humans and trolls to work this out.

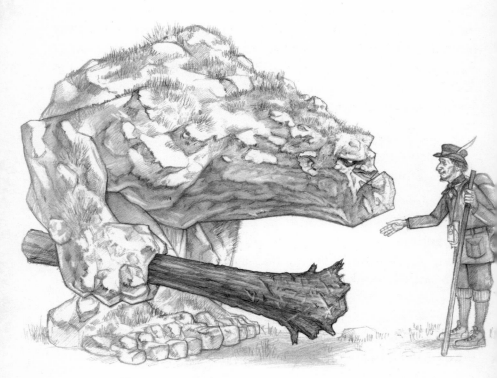

Most trolls you are likely to meet understand this now, but if upon meeting a troll you can find it in you to hit him as hard as you can on the chin, you will have a friend for life and also someone to carry you to the nearest bonesetter.

If invited to dine with trolls, you must remember that there is very little that trolls and humans can both eat. Trolls can enjoy some human foods, merely for the flavour, but they can't digest them properly and they don't have much food value for trolls. Thoughtful trolls will provide food suitable for humans. I'd better warn you, though, that trolls have only one word for vegetables and one word for meat. If they've known humans for some time they'll probably recognize that 'oak tree' and 'cabbage' are different, and so are 'cow' and 'frog'. What I'm delicately alludin' to here is that you'll get something organic, and probably heated. After that, you're on your own.

Trolls in the wild generally wear just a loincloth in order to have somewhere to hang knives and similar. In towns they've mostly adapted to wearing clothes of a sort, although this causes a few difficulties because male trolls find the sight of female trolls in large amounts of clothing very . . . interesting. I hear where there are places in Ankh-Morpork where lady trolls do a dance that *ends up* with them wearin' seven very thick blankets, by which time the gentleman trolls are breaking up the furniture and whistlin'.

If you invite trolls to dinner, settle for the loincloth.

PIXIES

AMONG THE CLANS OF THE PIXIES OR, AS THEY PREFER, THE PICTSIES, IT'S considered good etiquette to invite the whole of another clan to a huge banquet and then slaughter them all when they're drunk. Of course, this plan never works, because *no* pictsie is going to go to a banquet and lay off the drink, even if his chieftain has told him to stand by for some butchering later on, so what usually happens is that you get two roaring drunk mobs trying to slaughter one another and missing. A perfectly ordinary feast, in other words.

It is said that, if you leave a saucer of milk out for the pictsies, they will break into your cottage and steal everything in your drinks cabinet.

ETIQUETTE WITH SCARECROWS

THIS MAY BE A BIT STRANGE, AND ONLY APPLIES IN LANCRE. IN FACT, it only really applies to Unlucky Charlie.

Unlucky Charlie was made many years ago as a sort of target for use in the Witch Trials*, and has been blown up, blown apart, sent flying and generally magically mangled for years.

What we did not realize in them days, of course, is that if you keep throwin' magic at something, some of it sticks.

There is something scary about scarecrows, in any case. I know that's their job, but I mean scarier even than that. They're not exactly people but they're not exactly just... stuff. Or maybe it's those cut-out eyes.

Unlucky Charlie moves about. No one has ever seen how he does it. He might turn up in your garden, or right under the front of the window. You might come down of a morning and there he is standin' by the fire. I once found him in my bedroom, still on his stake.

The important thing is not to make a fuss or rush about, and certainly not to touch him. You can say things like 'Good morning, Unlucky Charlie,' or 'You're looking very frightening today, Unlucky Charlie.' If there's a meal and he's in the room, put out a portion for Unlucky Charlie. He won't eat any, but some people say that he rustles a bit, which might mean he's sayin' thank you although it could be just mice.

---

*A general get-together when witches from all the Ramtops come and meet in a typical witchy atmosphere of sisterhood and goodwill (i.e., all nice smiles over the top of a seethin' mass of envy, scurrilous gossip and general touchiness – I *like* the Trials). The witches show off tricks and spells developed during the year in a spirit of friendly co-operation (har har) to see who is going to come second to Granny Weatherwax, although of course this is all in fun and not a serious contest (I can hardly keep a straight face even when writin' this down). And there's a bonfire afterwards, and more gossip. In the bad old days, my own granny told me, a real person was sometimes used instead of Unlucky Charlie, but witches ain't like that any more. Well, most of them ain't. Some of 'em, anyway. Me, at least.

It is quite all right to dry clothes on him, because Unlucky Charlie likes to be useful. But remember to take them off him before you go to bed, otherwise they'll be gone in the morning and so will he.

People say that if Unlucky Charlie comes to your house and feels he's been well treated you'll get a monster crop of pumpkins next year, *even if you didn't plant any seeds.*

Do not play tricks on him, or stay up to watch him leave. A few people have tried it and they've been found very deeply asleep the next morning and, for ever afterwards, a little bit quiet and very reticent on the whole subject of straw.

Rules of Precedence

THESE CAN BE very tryin' for even the most experienced hostess. Now, of course, the way to start would be to tell you how to address dukes and counts but, you know, you can go for *days* without ever havin' an earl to dinner. Anyway, your *genuine* aristocrat swears worse than my granny and never bothers with a napkin if there's a footman to wipe his hands on. I used to work up the Palace when I was a girl when they used to have visitin' nobs of all kinds. I could tell you stories (but I won't because gossip is not in my nature). Let's just say I could've been a duchess ... well, *technic'ly* ... if I hadn't been quicker on my feet.

For your average party, the rules of precedence run like this:

> Witches (this is automatic, and witches sit where they like).
>
> Someone who has brought a whole bottle of whisky with a name you recognize.
>
> Someone who has brought a whole bottle of whisky with a name you recognize, but which, on closer examination, is spelled wrong (this is definitely a sign that you shouldn't spill any on the carpet).
>
> Someone who can play a musical instrument really well while drunk.
>
> Someone who has brought any kind of bottle of drink (if it's a second-hand bottle with an old cork hammered in halfway, though, have a care. Some of the very best drink comes out of the deep woods in second-hand bottles. Have a sniff. If your eyes water, you have a new friend).
>
> Someone who can play a musical instrument really well while sober.
>
> Anyone with any interestin' gossip.*
>
> Anyone who can do interestin' tricks, like makin' faces through a toilet seat or farting in tunes (people always remember my parties, often for years).
>
> Everyone else.

*I always say: if you haven't got anything good to say about anyone, say it to me.

See how sensible this is? Even if you're a duke, unless you brought a bottle or know all the verses of the dirty version of 'Where Has All The Custard Gone?' you're *nobody* at one of my *swaries*. I was once at a posh do in Ankh-Morpork and there was one man there everyone was bowin' and scrapin' to and, you know, he didn't sing a single comic song? He didn't even bring a bottle and even *trolls* know to bring a bottle. Some people have no idea how to behave, in my opinion.

Modes of Address

A LOT OF MY old etiquette books make a big thing about this and really it boils down to a few simple rules.

When you are dealin' with armed men, or people who *employ* armed men, there is no time to wonder if you are dealing with the second son of a viscount or whatever. No. What you are dealing with is *edged weapons*, and edged weapons are always addressed as 'sir'. Or even 'my lord'. All edged weapons care about is that you know what you are in the scheme of things, i.e., something easily cut.

After that it's all a lot simpler. Gen'rally speaking, how you address other people depends on you. The kind of people who fret if they're called 'your graciousness' instead of 'your sire-ness' aren't worth knowing. I always find 'Wotcha, how's your belly off for spots?' and a good slap on the back works nine times out of ten.

Contrary to what you might believe, calling someone 'friend' or 'pal' is not considered friendly or pally. Nor is an inquiry as to whether their mother can sew.

Etiquette at the Table

SOONER OR LATER, as my advice helps you rise through society like a bubble of marsh gas, you will find yourself lookin' at a table covered in glasses (if you're looking at a table covered in glass, you have probab'ly strayed into one of those bars I mentioned earlier and it is time to call someone 'sir'). There will also be more cutlery around your plate than your mother owned.

The advice used to be to start with the eating irons that are on the outside, but some butlers have got wise to this and have taken to movin' them around for a laugh. However, you can use this to your advantage 'cos no one knows the right ones to choose. So pick anything that looks useful and act with confidence. The chances are that the rest of the table will meekly join you and they'll be eating their soup with the teaspoons as if they'd meant to all along. I have to say, though, that the posher the dinner the fiddlier the food, and so you'll be one up on everybody if you learn to use the more difficult cutlery – asparagus tongs, pea shooters, parsnip spears and the like. They'll be useful for these tricky foods.

Artichokes:— The ideal slimming food, as the effort of fiddling with and eating them uses up far more calories than they contain. You tear off each leaf individually, dip the fleshy end in the sauce and then scrape the soft part off with your teeth. Place the uneaten portion tidily on the side of your plate, although it is permissible to flick it into the lampshade. Artichokes were invented because rich people didn't have enough to do with their time.

Asparagus:— Only ever eat these with your left hand, and never use a knife and fork, otherwise bluebirds will fly out of your nose. You dip the tip into the sauce, and then flip the end into your mouth using the asparagus flipper. Eat only the soft part – it is very vulgar to polish off every bit, however hungry you are. Since asparagus does some odd things to the digestion I'm amazed it's posh to eat, but it's probably because it's hard to grow.

Bread:— Again, use your left hand. Never bite pieces off your bread. Instead tear off little bite-sized pieces and pop them in individually, buttering them first, on a side plate, if preferred. If a fool or jester is employed, it is in order to throw rolls at him underarm.

Butter:— This will be displayed in pats on a separate dish. Take one pat and put it on your bread plate. Don't spread straight from the butter plate, because it will poison you.

Caviar:— The nobby way to eat caviar is from the little pad on the outside of your left hand, between your forefinger and thumb. However, since people also take snuff in a very similar way it is important not to get confused. It is not the noseful of fish eggs that is the problem, it is trying to pretend that you meant it.

The much less etiquette way is to eat the caviar with accompaniments like chopped egg, onion and lemon juice.

But the real way to eat caviar is with a ladle and a glass of the sort of drink that turns into vapour an inch from your lips.

Cheese:— It is usual, when helping yourself from the cheeseboard, to endeavour to leave the cheese in a tidy and usable state for the next person. No one likes an untidy cheese. Use the cheese knife.

Corn on the cob:—In posh houses you'll be given two forks to skewer either end of the cob. Others will expect you to hold it with your fingers. However you eat it you will get bits of corn stuck in your teeth, which will provide oral exercise and a snack for later in the evening. If you need to remove your false teeth during this meal, do it politely behind a napkin. Do not do the 'gottle o' gear' routine, because no one ever laughs.

Fish:— It is now acceptable to eat fish with a knife and fork (instead of two forks, as used to be the accepted method; the use of the fish rammer has quite died out). Fillet as you go and never turn the fish over. If you do find yourself with a fishbone in your mouth, this should be spat into your left hand and placed on the side of your plate. Never use your fingers. If you are choking to death, nod respectfully to your host as you lose consciousness.

The cherry problem:— People say to me, 'Mrs Ogg, how do you eat cherries and prunes and other things with stones when you're in posh company?' And I shall tell you.

Eat these whole, spitting the stones into your left hand and discreetly depositing them on the side of your plate, even if an inviting target presents itself somewhere else on the table. However, if the hostess has had the foresight to provide cherry-stone shooters, and indicates that these may now be used by delicately pinging one off the head of a guest at the other end of the table, much simple merriment may be enjoyed.

Most countries have some equivalent to 'Tinker, Tailor, Soldier, Sailor', and it is in my opinion perfectly all right to swallow a few stones in order to square yourself with whatever profession you wish. What does a burst appendix matter if you get the job you want? It is not etiquette to nick a couple off a neighbour's plate in order to improve your prospects, but it is allowable to sell him some if you have some to spare.

Royalty are also allowed to count their stones publicly, although of course the rhyme for them can only be 'King, King, King, King, King, King, King, King' (or 'Queen'), which does not make for much in the way of dramatic tension over the custard.

Oysters:— These should only be eaten on a day with a 'y' in it. They'll be served raw in their shells. You squeeze lemon over 'em and then just pour 'em down your throat. The sensation is a bit like having a bad cold and no handkerchief. And that's about it for oysters. They're much better if you cook them with a bit of bacon, because then they taste of bacon.

Pasta:— Eat this with a fork, never a fork and spoon. Place the fork vertically on the plate and twist around a small portion of spaghetti, pulling to the side of your plate. Some big houses now boast a set of clockwork spaghetti forks, which can reduce the effort required.

Peas:— In polite circles in Ankh-Morpork (and these are pretty small circles), peas are squashed onto the top side of the pea fork for conveying into the educated mouth. In Quirm, it is acceptable to blow them onto one side of the plate by means of a special straw.

Snails:— Most people rely on thrushes to dispose of these garden pests, but they are still considered a delicacy in Quirm. Much of the Quirm diet developed during a twenty-year siege, when the population scoffed its way through the entire contents of the zoo and were then reduced to turning over damp stones and hitting with a hammer anything that moved. Snails are eaten directly from their shells. Apparently there's something called a snail fork, but I don't see how they could hold one.

Soup:— Always move the spoon away from you when picking up soup. You are allowed to bring it towards your mouth once the spoon is full. The bowl, too, should be tilted away from you when you are spooning up the last drops. This is one of those bits of etiquette that makes sense. No one likes a lapful of hot soup. Ask anyone.

Tea and coffee:— What to do when the tea or coffee is too hot is one of those little problems that crop up all the time. The correct way to deal with it is to put it into the saucer and fan it gently with your hat, while continuing to make polite conversation.

Alcohol:— It is scarcely necessary to remark that drinking too much wine is very bad etiquette indeed, my word yes. At one time it was actually fashionable to become intoxicated after dinner, but those days are gone, I am thankful to say. The wineglass is never drained at a draught in polite society (but see the section on Dwarf etiquette), nor should you wipe your mouth with your hand. That tablecloth is there for a *reason*.

'PORT AND CIGARS'

THERE IS A LOT OF MISUNDERSTANDING ABOUT THE WHOLE BUSINESS of 'port and cigars'. After a high-class meal in some societies it is considered etiquette for the ladies to leave, but if you don't go no one seems to make you and you get some decent brandy and cigars plus perhaps a few jokes you haven't heard before.

Incidentally, when offered port you should say, 'Ah, yes, I will have a little port.' Everyone says this. You have to say it even if what you intend is a *lot* of port.

The port wine is always passed round to the left (to port). The problem is that if you miss the port as it passes you, on account of perhaps you are lighting another cigar or trying to think up a new joke, it is very bad form to ask for it to be passed back. The rules say you should pass your empty glass to the left so that it can catch up with the decanter, be filled by the person holding the decanter and passed back to you.

Now, this can cause difficulties, because by then everyone

except you has been drinking the port, and what with one thing or another you can find that your glass moves around the table slower than the port and the decanter gets back to you before you get your glass back. It's not good manners to hang on to it until your glass catches up, because people downstream from you will be dying of thirst.

I find the best way is to run around the table until you're ahead of the decanter, pull the chair out from under some other diner, and be sitting there ready when the port comes past. I've done this several times and there's been no complaints, so it's probably good manners.

Smoking

BEFORE SMOKIN' IN a strange house, I always feel it is a good idea to ask people around you if they mind you doing so. Anything less than a threat to kill you if you light up should be considered a 'no'. After all, the world is full of fools, and you are not allowed to object to that, even though passive stupidity kills so many people.

If you are stayin' in a house where they *will* kill you if you smoke, it is etiquette to smoke lying on your back in your room with your head in the hearth and blowin' the smoke up the chimney.

When smokin' in company, it is very bad luck to light three cigarettes with one match because the third smoker will be shot by a concealed sniper. Some people make such a fuss about a little smoke.

Be very wary around creepy signs that say 'Thank You For Not Smoking', because there's magic afoot. Otherwise, how did they know you wouldn't?

Some Notes on Gardening

PEOPLE SAY TO me: 'Mrs Ogg, should we sow our parsnips when the moon is waxing or when the moon is waning?' They say: 'If it rains on Soul Cake Tuesday, should we plant our early beans?' They say: 'Is it true that onion beds shouldn't be weeded after the 1st of August?'

And I say: the hell with it. Witches knows about herbs, because that makes sense, and the good thing about most herbs is that they grow all by themselves. You just go for a walk with your eye to business and there they are (the really useful ones, anyway; the ones you mostly see growing in gardens are only useful for shoving up a chicken's bottom). But witches don't garden. Gardening involves digging in cold weather. Where's the fun in that? And the rest of the time you're mostly trying to kill something.

What witches cultivate is *people*. It takes a lot less work to get friendly with a few keen gardeners and then, from about July onwards, you won't be able to move for free runner beans, tomatoes, courgettes the size of marrows and more rhubarb than was ever meant to happen. They love givin' the stuff away. It makes 'em feel proud. And it's good manners to respect other people's feelings. That's etiquette, that is.

Births

IN LANCRE WE don't go in for announcements about birth because everyone knows it's going to happen, sometimes before the young lady concerned, and in any case a lot of her mum's friends will be hangin' around the house or just popping in for a cupful of gossip on the likely day and I don't have to tell you that by nightfall there *may* be lonely shepherds up on the hills who don't know everything about the birth, but I pers'nally doubt it.

However, these days young girls are findin' out what it's like outside Lancre, so it seems nothing will do but they've got to have at least a big sign on the door saying something like:

IT'S A BOY!

or

IT'S A GIRL!

or, in places like Slice and other parts of the Ramtops that are a bit backward in many ways:

IT'S A BABY!

(because I could tell you a few stories, but it is not in my nature).

Other details may be added as required, viz., how much the baby weighs, what time exactly it happened, when the wedding is, and so on. Of course, in posher places with a town cryer and so on you can go further and compose hum'rous announcements like:

> 'We have an extra Peckweather! Bettina has bounced into the home of Bertie and Claribelle Lusillon Ironpurse-Peckweather. Bettina arrived at twenty-four minutes after three on the afternoon of 15 Grune. She weighed 7lbs 2oz and was delivered by Goodie Rattle!'

But in my opinion this is a horrible start to give to any baby.

It is traditional to give a large bottle of rum to the midwife afterwards, if she is me. Another bit of etiquette to remember is to make sure the older female relatives are out of earshot, because the last thing a young woman needs at a time like this is some old neighbour rattlin' on mournfully about the terrible time she had with her eldest, who came out sideways playing a trombone, or something.

NAMING CEREMONIES, PRESENTS
AND OTHER MATTERS
(including special considerations for those in a magical environment)

FIRSTLY, WISE PARENTS SHOULD MAKE SURE THEY'VE READ ANY BOOKS of folktales that might be around. Those stories weren't just made up, you know. They are there for your protection. Learn from history. Calling a girl Beauty or Rose Red or Shining Eyes is just asking for trouble. Don't go boasting to any kings about how beautiful she is. Incident'ly, if when she grows up she turns out to be able to spin flax into gold, my advice is to *keep very quiet about it*. A good move is to buy an old gold mine and then let on that you've struck lucky. A little forethought is all it needs.

However, it is okay to let your daughter be a milkmaid and sing sweetly where any kings can hear, and encouraging her not to complain about the fit of any shoes she might be asked to put on by men in powdered wigs may stand her in good stead in later life. Trust me on this one.

If you *are* a king your daughter will be beautiful. People have tried all kinds of aids to beauty, like washing in the morning dew, shoving yoghurt on their faces, etc, but for my money the best way to be beautiful is to have a dad with a lot of money and a bunch of armed men. It's just amazin' how people will spontaneously see what a beautiful princess you are in those circumstances.

There's a lot of little kings along the Ramtops, and they're always sayin' to me, 'Mrs Ogg, how do you stand on golden balls?' And, you know, this is a tricky one. You just *know* what's going to happen if you give

133

a princess a golden ball. She'll lose it down the nearest well, and then a talkin' frog will turn up, and the next thing you know is you've got a son-in-law who . . . well, yes, he's a handsome prince, and I'll grant you that these are not to be sneezed at, but frankly you wouldn't want to see his family turn up at the wedding and anyway if they did they'd probably be in a jar.

I gen'rally cut through the whole thing by pointing out that gold is a very stupid thing to make a ball out of. They never bounce no matter how hard you throw them.

Boys is easier, and if you have sons it's worth trying for three. That sets the third one up nicely to marry any spare princesses that are around when he's grown up. If he can get a job as a swineherd, so much the better. It'd only be temp'ry. As Esmerelda Weatherwax always says, the stories are out there and it's up to you to leap on 'em as they go past (however, you can't bet on it. F'r'instance, when my boys was young I was always sending 'em off to take cows to market, and usually by the time they got back I'd always got a seed bed dug for any magical seeds they might have accepted, but all they ever brought home was a big handful of money. I must have slipped up somewhere).

Presents for the new baby need some thought. What Mum wants is a big bag of nappies, someone to do the washing and a nice long holiday somewhere far away from her husband. What she'd probably have to settle for is a bunch of flowers and in posher households a silver teething ring for the baby. Of course, it's help-ful to her if you remember to give something to the other children in the family, who might be put out and gen'rally whining about the new member, so what I give them is a thick ear unless they promise to shut up right *now*.

On the subject of presents, in these rural areas where natural magic is still pretty strong, I ort to mention the treatment of any witches or godmothers in the area.

What everyone hopes for, certainly, is a few of the nicer sort of witch or even a genuine godmother who'll be free with the Health, Wealth and Happiness business, but it is vit'ly important not to leave out any of the touchier witches that might live in the vicinity, other-wise someone'll screech 'Ahhahaha!' in the middle of the ceremony and the next thing you know is you'll be up to your neck in poisoned spinnin' wheels. After all, how hard is it to invite her along, give her plenty to drink and a plate of ham rolls all to herself and keep her out of the way of your posh auntie? Play your cards right and you could be ahead by one extra good wish. She may be a bit whiffy on the nose, but it's better than waking up a hundred years later and findin' trees have grown up through the floor. A bit of forethought is all it takes.

Courtship

IT MAY COME as a surprise that anyone needs any instructions about this, but even I was once a rather shy girl who had difficulty meeting young men. But it wore off by mid-morning when I realized what I was doing wrong.

The hardest part is striking up a conversation, but it is easy if you take your time and look for the right opportunity. My first husband was very good at this. We met because he was doing some digging for my dad, sweating away with his shirt off, and I wouldn't be givin' away any secrets if I said I found plenty of opportunity to nip up to the log pile (which in these parts we always put right by the privy, so as to kill two birds with one stone). It was a hot day, but I don't reckon we ever had such a good fire going. Anyway, he looked up at me as I went up there for the tenth time and quick as a flash, I shall always remember, he said, 'Got the runs 'ave yer?'

There you have it – just the right comment at the right time. Also, it made me laugh so much I dropped a log on my foot and he had to help me indoors. After that, one thing led to another and *he*'s called Jason.

I never see the lad with his shirt off on a hot day without thinking of his dad. Of course, we've all passed a lot of water since then.

ON PRESSING YOUR SUIT

YOUNG MEN SAY TO ME, 'MRS OGG, WHEN A YOUNG MAN HAS honourable intentions towards a young lady, how should he go about pressing his suit?'

And I think it is a good thing that a would-be swain thinks about this, because it's prob'ly the first time in his life he's ever had to worry where the ironing board is. It's best to try it out on an old shirt or two, unless going courting with brown arrow shapes all over your suit is fashionable in your part of the world. Once you've got the temperature right, it's time to try pressing the suit itself. Oddly enough, it's often the trousers that give trouble. Sideways creases do not impress, but I remember when our Jason first pressed *his* suit he managed to get four creases per leg, and the boxy look caught on around here for a while.

That's what I know about pressing your suit.

137

ON GIRLS MAKING ADVANCES

SOMETIMES GIRLS AND WOMEN PLAN EVENTS WITH A DIRECT VIEW to scraping an acquaintance with young men. Dropping something is an obvious way, although in public this is usually a parcel or sunshade.

It says in my old etiquette book: 'It is scarcely necessary to say that girls who stoop to this kind of manoeuvring are hardly ever gentlewomen. It cannot be denied that girls of the lower middle classes are prone to it. A gentleman should hesitate before choosing as a wife a girl who shows so little discretion as to walk and talk with young men of whom she knows nothing beyond what they choose to tell her.'

Well, in Lancre no lad looking for a wife who can help with the harvest is going to have much interest in a girl who can't pick up her own sunshade. If a little parcel is going to give her much trouble, she's going to be no good with a couple of buckets of milk, either. In fact it has been known for young men to drop a bale of hay in the road near the young lady's cottage to see if she'll pick it up. Any girl who'll pass up the opportunity of free hay isn't likely to be a provident wife, they say.

We breed good men in Lancre, but I have to say sometimes they could do with a good ding around the lughole.

OFFERING AN UMBRELLA

MY OLD ETIQUETTE BOOK ALSO SAYS: 'IT IS ETIQUETTE TO OFFER an unknown lady an umbrella in the street, supposing she stood in need of one. No lady would accept the offer from a stranger; and the other sort of female might never return the umbrella. In large towns women of breeding soon learn to view casual attentions from well-dressed men with the deepest distrust.'

However, my advice is: it's better to make the acquaintance of a kind man than die of pneumonia. Person'ly, I've always enjoyed casual attentions. You might get a good dinner out of them. A lady is always polite, appreciative, and carries a horseshoe in her handbag. This is not for luck: the added weight can come in handy.

CHAPERONES

IN LANCRE IT IS GENERALLY CONSIDERED ETIQUETTE TO HAVE A responsible female relative within two miles of the young couple at all times.

In remote areas, and they don't get much more remote than up here, the age-old practice of 'bundling' is still, er, practised. On long cold winter nights, when the young man may have come a long way, he is allowed to share a bed with the young lady, although both remain fully clothed and a bolster is put down the middle. However, since love traditionally laughs at locksmiths, it probably grins widely at a pillow full of feathers.

A NOTE ABOUT LOVE LETTERS

ONCE AGAIN, THIS IS AN AREA WHERE A BIT OF THOUGHT RIGHT NOW can save some red faces later on. Women have this habit of saving up billets of doux and tyin' them up with a ribbon and keeping them in a drawer somewhere and, sure enough, about ten years later you finds that the kids have dug them out and are reading them to their friends for a penny a time. Once again, a bit of foresight now can work wonders. With a bit of co-operation between the writers it's wise to begin the missives like this:

'My dearest love,
GET YOUR HANDS OFF OF THIS, YOU THIEVING DEVILS!
YES, WE KNOW IT'S YOU! PUT THEM BACK THIS MINUTE!'

Of course, it helps even more if you've discussed early on what names you're going to give your children when you have them. This will then earn you an entire quiet afternoon while they try to work out how you did it, and possibly also give them one of them complexes which will benefit them in later life.

This is also a good time to mention:

THE SIGNIFICANCE OF STAMPS

THIS GOES BACK TO THE DAYS WHEN ANY LETTER THAT ARRIVED IN the house was read by *everyone* and girls weren't allowed to have private correspondence until they were thirty-five.

When the stamp is in the centre at the top it signifies an affirmative answer to the question (we won't go into what the question might be), and when it is at the bottom, it is a negative. Should the stamp be on the right-hand corner, at an angle, it asks the question if the receiver of the letter loves the sender; in the left-hand corner it means the writer hates the other. If it is in the middle of the letter, it has covered the address, so the letter will be delivered to the wrong house but will make for interestin' reading and you'll get strange looks from the neighbours.

If there is no stamp you'll have to pay the postie. This means it is a very bad start to a relationship.

The Lancre Love Seat

IN TIMES OF yore, when a young man wished to show his young lady that he was of a mind to get serious and set up house with her, he would start to work upon the site of their new home.

The first act, so that he and his fellow workers (usually his family and friends) would have some facilities, would be to dig the privy. As time went on, this act became more symbolic and the young man would carve for his paramour an ornate privy seat. The carvings would include the name of the young lady and her swain, along with the usual flurry of hearts, cherubs and doves. Of course, this made them uncomfortable, but comfort has never been a big consideration when it comes to the realms of Amour, otherwise boned corsets would never have been invented.

The seats are now often carved in miniature, to be carried in a pocket or bag. Really skilled beaux carve the seats (or have them carved by dwarf craftsmen) so tiny that they can be used as pendants. These miniature seats are highly prized even in the élite circles of Ankh-Morpork, and an antique example made by skilled dwarf craftsmen can fetch thousands of dollars. Less exalted versions are often used as frames for mirrors, and are considered extremely risible.

Balls

(how to behave at them)

IT IS A truth self evident that a man in possession of his own teeth, a decent pair of boots, a couple of acres of land and some pigs that need feeding must be in want of a wife. Balls are a good way to meet one. That's why they're held. The dancing is just a way of passing the time, something for you to do while your mind is on other things. Even up in the Ramtops there is the occasional big ball, and these require a level of etiquette rather higher than your average village hop or hoe-down, where the key thing is to remember to go outside if you need to throw up.

Firstly you should, of course, reply to the invitation as soon as you receive it. It will say RSVP, and you must reservup. Put some effort into it. Your host or hostess has gone to the trouble of putting runny writing and gold edging on the card, so a decently spelled letter is the least you can do. Balls cost a lot to put on. Even if you're royal, it's good manners to let people know you're coming – in fact *especially* if you're royal, because nothing flusters people so much as an unexpected king.

The only exception to this rule, in the Ramtops, is witches. Witches just turn up, or not. It's accepted that they have all sorts of calls on their time.

If it says 8 p.m. on the card, and you believe it, you'll find yourself the only guest. Even though you do get a good crack at the drink before anyone else arrives, it's still not good manners. A good hostess will employ a few people to be 'early guests', so as the first real arrivals won't feel embarrassed (this is a good earner for anyone who can wear evening dress and doesn't have ears that stick out too much; you get some free drinks, all the canapés you can stuff in your pocket and a dollar for your trouble besides).

She will introduce you to other guests and, as a result, you may get much of your dance card filled. I've always thought these things were a bit pompous, but it's etiquette once again. It's considered good manners to dance with the host or hostess, and also any maiden aunts or surviving grandparents who will want to get out on the floor – and I've known elderly ladies who're still capable of dancing at 2 a.m. when a succession of their young partners have been helped out onto the balcony for some fresh air. The important thing is to keep your feet moving. Some of the steps are bound to be right.

It's also good manners to circulate and not just hang around the people you came with. A good tip here, I find, is to keep your eye on the people carrying trays of drinks and food. Keep up with them. The evening will pass very happily.

To young men I would say: you've prob'ly been invited because you can dance and are known to wash regular, so make yourself available to dance with any plain neglected wallflower. She may be spotty, but what is a sky without stars?

Incident'ly, in etiquettable circles it's not done to dance with anyone for more than two dances in succession unless you're engaged to them. Also, it's a good idea to have some non-controversial smalltalk ready. 'I don't know about you, but I'm really sweaty,' is not suitable, whereas 'Don't you think it is a trifle warm in here?' is fine and, of course, invites agreement that perhaps a stroll on the verandah is in order. What could be more enjoyable than to sit in some cool retreat with a charming girl? Well, quite a lot, but some of it starts right there, just my little joke.

If you play your cards right and are seen out on the dance floor entering into the spirit of the thing, you will find yourself a favourite with hostesses and, if you take care to fill your pockets with loose nibbles, you might not have to buy any food for several months.

It is very bad manners to accept an invitation to a dance if you cannot dance. If you do, you may take the place of another who is more accomplished and your incompetence will make you a waste of space. Learn. Take professional lessons. Most of the steps are pretty easy, and the more understanding hostesses won't mind you painting 'L' and 'R' on your shoes.

We can't leave the subject of courtship without mentioning:

The Language of Flowers

THIS IS SOMETHING that has died out in recent years, which is a shame, but you can see why when you read about the scandal. It all seemed so romantic until then.

Of course, these days all people remember is 'rosemary for remembrance' and a few odds and ends like that, but when the vogue was in its heyday there were more than nine hundred different items of vegetation (trees and even some vegetables as well as flowers) with their own meanings. In a way they were very much like naval signal flags, which can either have their own meaning ('Ship invaded by strange creatures in a metal saucer, am abandoning lunch'), or simply be a number or letter of the alphabet, depending on how they're used. To put it another way, you could use vegetation to say *anything*.

Those of you with a freewheeling type of mind can see that here was an accident just waiting to happen.

Down in Sto Lat, for example, there was old Mr Gladdybone, who was, how can I put it, the sort of old gentleman who sniggers when he sees a lady's washing blowing in the wind. And down the lane lived Miss Mellifera Buster, who was something of a folklorist, and who was the first person ever to try to get the constables to prosecute someone for having an obscene garden.

She said she particularly objected to the Creeping Shrillflower, but planting it between the Love-Lies-Panting and the begonias was the last straw. Also, when she com-plained, the old man had waved an artichoke at her and talked about the hardy perennial Scarlet Bellweed, a flower she had never expected ever to hear on the lips of a man old enough to be her older brother.

She also considered the planting of peas and leeks in his back garden, easily seen from her bedroom win-dow if you knelt on top of the wardrobe, was not as innocent as it seemed, considering the proximity of Nettle-leaved Forthright and Toad Spurge.

Then the old tree stump at the front of his garden had put forth a crop of Maiden's Puzzle, an unusual fungus, and since the old man had planted Old Maids Aplenty all round it she hoped she didn't have to explain to anyone what *that* meant.

The case went on for a long time and caused a lot of interest, especially since most people until then hadn't had a clue about the code. It turned out, for example, that the famous painting *Still Life with Blue Flowers* by Augustine Simnel, prints of which turn up everywhere, was really a very unpleasant attack on his mother-in-law if the blooms were read clockwise. As for the floral walk which Lord Ouida had planted through his estate after he'd been forced to re-open an ancient footpath, well, mothers used to cover their children's eyes after they got past the rhododendrons. Mind you, that man was a Creeping Foxglove/Mouse Cress/Climbing Elderberry/Water Dropwort, and his father was no better.

The madness died away after a while, although not before a particularly obscene hedge was torn down, and I suppose it was because of that that the whole language of flowers folklore was forgotten. There was also some talk that Miss Buster had made up some of the dirtier ones, particularly the one about the Ragged-leaved Trefoil, which I didn't even understand until I was thirty. And I still can't see a dandelion without grinnin'.

I did hear that some time afterwards Miss Buster married Mr Gladdybone, but I expect life was no bed of roses.

Here are some pretty flowers and their meanings:

Memo from J.H.C. Goatberger
To: Thos. Cropper, overseer

I knew this would happen! Every single meaning she gives is highly suggestive, except the one she gives for peonies! Get rid of them all!

Memo from Thos. Cropper
To: J.H.C. Goatberger, publisher

I'm afraid the one for peonies is also obscene, sir.

Memo from J.H.C. Goatberger
To: Thos. Cropper, overseer

Is it? I thought it was rather charming.

Memo from Thos. Cropper
To: J.H.C. Goatberger, publisher

I'm afraid so, sir. I have removed the whole section.

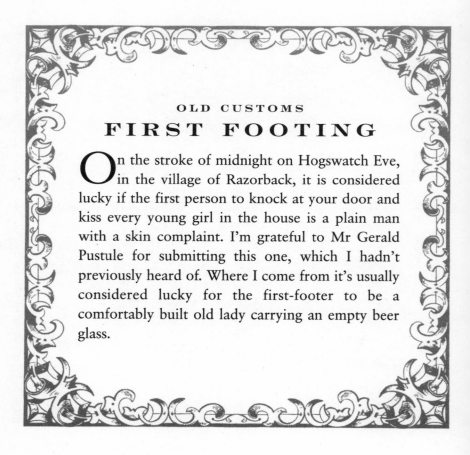

FIRST FOOTING

On the stroke of midnight on Hogswatch Eve, in the village of Razorback, it is considered lucky if the first person to knock at your door and kiss every young girl in the house is a plain man with a skin complaint. I'm grateful to Mr Gerald Pustule for submitting this one, which I hadn't previously heard of. Where I come from it's usually considered lucky for the first-footer to be a comfortably built old lady carrying an empty beer glass.

MAKING POTPOURRI

Nothin' gives a home that etiquettable look so much as bowls of potpourri. Now, traditionally, the way to make this is with lavender, rosebuds, cloves and other such stuff, which has to be dried, and mostly you end up with something grey that's frankly a touch musty. And people will look up their noses at you because it's not the right colour and smell.

The proper way is as follows.

YOU NEED

anything dry — twigs, wood shavings, unlucky frogs, bits of old beetle
some brightly coloured paints
some cheap scent

Paint the dry stuff and scatter scent on it. That's all they do to make the expensive stuff you see in shops, after all.

Marriage

ENGAGEMENTS

EVEN IN THESE MODERN TIMES YOUNG PEOPLE STILL DO LIKE to go through the motions before marriage and sometimes they even get engaged (just my little joke). As my old dad used to say: 'If you think being engaged is fun, just wait 'til you're married. In fact, please wait until you're married'.* I always think our dad didn't get out much, and it was a good job he was a bit deaf.

People say to me, 'Mrs Ogg, who should be the one to propose marriage?' and generally I don't see that it matters if it's the boy or the girl, but things have been let slide a little if it has to be the girl's father. Arranged marriages are still pretty common in these parts (and now I come to think of it, what other kinds are there? It's not as if the boy and the girl and all their relatives and a new dress and the priest of choice and a slap-up knife-and-fork tea for forty all turn up in one place by accident, is it?). I'm talking about the kind where an observant mum has a word with her daughter and then with the mum of the boy, and then both dads get told, and it's generally agreed that a wedding within the next few months would be a good idea. I've known plenty of good old marriages that began that way, and at least it reduces the element of surprise all round.

But in a nutshell there's a lot of agonizing about this and it doesn't matter at all. Marriage isn't something someone does to someone else. It's perfectly all right if the woman asks, it ain't like it's begging. The important thing is to know the answer in advance.

Whoever does the asking between the couple, the young man should then ask the bride's father, but this is okay because first the girl has an informal word with her mum to make sure it's sorted

*This joke was dug out of a peat bog, and is prob'ly a thousand years old.

out all right. It's really more of a way to get the old man to shell out for new dresses all round but he'll probably hurrumph a bit and, as they say, seek reassurance that the young man has the wherewithal to support his daughter, because it's v. embarrassing to rent out the attic bedroom and then find she's back on the doorstep two weeks later. The swain will also get asked if he has any other 'expectations'. It is not polite to raise any points about the girl's expectations at this point.

It is usual to have a bit of a party once an engagement's been announced. This used to be so that the two families could get the measure of one another and see if any special weapons will need to be brought to the wedding, but things are a bit more civilized now (see Fights, later on). It is not a good idea to bring along any of the more embarrassing relatives; save them until the wedding, by which time it's usually too late to run.

Lengths of Engagements:— Mostly engagements last no longer than six or seven months, but being engaged can become a habit. Take Yodel Lightly and Miss Conception Weaver, who were engaged for sixty-five years.

I suppose neither of them was much taken with the passions of the flesh, what with her being so skilled at lacemaking and, of course, he had his pigeons, but, as she always pointed out, it meant that things were sorted out. Most of the time, space being hard to come by, they were waiting for people to die – his old dad, her old mum, his old mum, her old dad – and then just waiting became a sort of habit. Then they died, on the same day; he fell off his pigeon loft and she got blood poisoning from a needle. Old Brother Perdore was a decent sort and had 'em buried in the same grave, just to prove that poets don't always know what they're talking about. I don't know what they're waiting for now.

The Ring:— This has got to be large and glittery, otherwise the girl will have to walk round with her hand extended in an awkwardly nonchalant fashion. They are usually non-returnable and it's not good manners to hand one over attached to a piece of elastic. My advice to a young man is not to spend a lot, beause it's the thought that counts. You can always say you're saving up for the new cottage or whatever, and anyway you might have to buy some more one day. I used to know a lady who had all her engagement rings made into a charm bracelet. This is not a cultured thing to do.

When to Marry:— By and large, it's still best to try and get through the ceremony before having a baby. On the more mundane topic of what time of the year and of the day to hold your wedding, it's good to aim for the warmer weather (so do think about that when planning any events that may require you to get married!) Also remember to avoid Octeday, which is sacred to the followers of the church of Offler; on that day they are not permitted to have any fun at all because the prophet Jeremanda once spent a bad Octeday during his holidays in Llamedos. As to time of the day, the meal after the ceremony is, of course, usually called the wedding breakfast. Logically, the service should be held around 8 a.m., which then allows most of the rest of the day for serious feasting, quaffing and falling down. Also, breakfast cereal is quite cheap.

THE WEDDING

The Bride:— By right and ancient tradition, the bride is the focal point of any wedding and her duties are largely to do with making sure that she and her attendants look good on the big day. She appoints her bridesmaids, pages and any other attendants that she may want (matrons of honour, for example).

By tradition, the bridesmaids are dressed in outfits that under normal circumstances they wouldn't be seen dead in, often with little floral headdresses, which they are then given as a present after the ceremony. The dress is consigned to the back of the wardrobe and forgotten about until ten years later, when her children need something to dress up in.

Invitations to be a bridesmaid should not be accepted lightly. Why does the bride need to be surrounded by attractively dressed young women, which might serve to remind the groom of what he's leaving behind? It's because there's safety in numbers. Any evil spirits hanging around to cause bad luck for the bride will get confused, or so the belief goes. If you pay careful attention to any wedding ceremony you'll see that a lot of those funny little extras, silver horseshoes and the like, are really there to keep the bride safe. Dangerous times, weddings. That's why I always advise inviting any friendly witches along and making sure they get plenty to drink. You'll be thankful in the long run.

The Groom:— The bridegroom chooses his best man and the ushers, whose job it is to keep the crowd quiet and confiscate the larger weapons. He has to pay for all the flowers and all the costs of the service itself (even if you're just jumping over the broomstick, which used to be the popular method in Lancre, it's best to remember that a broomstick costs money and also that the people holding it may become, through lack of money, so confused that they lift it up quickly just as the groom is going to jump).

The groom also has to buy presents for his and

his wife-to-be's attendants. Most important of all, he has to provide everything for their new home – including all linen, glass, plate, furniture, fixtures and fittings. Under a Ramtops tradition he also has to conclude his stag night by digging a new privy in the garden of his new home and throwing up into it.

The Bride's Parents:— The bride's parents have to pay for all food and drink (including the wedding cake) and any other costs connected with the 'breakfast' and the evening party (including floral displays). They pay for the bride's and bridesmaids' dresses and any clothes for other attendants. This can be expensive for a man blessed with many daughters, and is the downside of having someone to look after him when he starts to dribble. Traditionally, he also had to find the dowry. In the case of kings and so on this was sometimes a whole duchy or something, and I suppose for the really big royal families the happy couple would have to make a list, otherwise they'd end up, it always happens, with three very nearly identical baronies and no toast rack at all.

Best Man:— The best man has to marry the bride if the groom fails to turn up. He may or may not therefore have strong incentive for his other major task – making sure that the groom arrives looking smart and in reasonably good condition, and is vertical, or alive, or at least present.

This can be a challenging task, since he also has to organize the party the night before, the sole purpose of which is to see that the groom does not arrive looking smart, ekcetra, ekcetra. So apart from a good head for strong drink, he also needs to know, to within a few minutes, how long it'll take the groom to wake up, escape from the handcuffs, break out of the chickenhouse, remove all the boot polish (at least from visible areas) and hop all the way to the nuptial venue with both legs down one trouser.

The Bridesmaids:— Mainly there, as I said, to be occult decoys and, if carefully chosen by the bride, to make her look good by comparison. They carry posies provided by the groom, who also gives them each a small present as a token of thanks. It used to be the case that the groom was expected to actually chase and catch his bride on the big day. The groom's presents to the bridesmaids is a tradition dating back to when the groom used to bribe the bridesmaids to lure the bride to a location where he could catch her without too much effort. Personally, whenever I hear anyone say this, I always ment'ly add, 'That's what he thought.'

How to Have the Fight:— A fight is traditional at all Ramtops weddings, except those involving royalty, where the tradition is a small war.

Lots of people have asked me for advice about this. They say, 'Mrs Ogg, can you just rely on there bein' a fight?' And, yes, you gen'rally can. My advice is to make sure the drink is strong enough and that people are seated right to make it happen quite soon. That way you've got it over with and can get on with things without that naggin' feelin' that something's wrong. Once it starts, though, it's vital to see that it goes properly, viz:

Stage One: This is what some people call The Challenge. It starts as soon as people have a few drinks inside them and start to chatter, whereupon Man 1 will say, per'aps:

'What was that you said about our Lil?'

(This is only an example, of course. Other suitable challenges include: 'Hah, you wouldn't talk like that if you knew what our grandad told us about your mum,' and, if all else fails, 'That's my pint you're suppin'' (although this is considered pretty poor and suggests not much thought has gone into things).)

This will take us to Stage Two: The Question. Again, this is fairly formal, but Man 2 can choose between a number of inquiries, seekin' to ascertain as it might be whether Man 1 requires a faceful of dandruff/knuckle sandwich/a nose that touches his ears on both sides.

The men will circle one another three or four times, which should not be difficult by now since both parties will be findin' it a lot easier to walk in circles. The crowd at this point are permitted a number of witticisms and shouts of encouragement, such as, 'Kick him inna fork, our Sam!'

At this point one bystander, known as the Shover, will push one of the circling men towards the other (technic'ly this is *Stage Three*, which does not last long). This will result in some aimless flailin', but the first decently landed blow will result in *Stage Four: the Wives*. At a signal, the ladies associated with the men will each grab their partner and shout variants on 'You wait till I gets you 'ome, I can't let you out of my sight for five minutes!' Hitting the man over the head with handbags is ritual at this point or, if the reception has gone on for some time, a bottle may be substituted.

Stage Five begins when one of the ladies says to the other something on the lines of, 'I'm surprised you've got the nerve to show your face here, after what you did to Aunty Shipley!' and they then fall to fighting with rather more malign expertise than their menfolk, who bury their differences to separate the couple before something expensive gets broken.

The bride then cuts the cake.

WEDDING ANNIVERSARIES

I can never remember what each anniversary is signified by. I asked around among my friends and people seem to agree on the following:

FIRST	soot or coal
SECOND	lacy privy stationery holder
THIRD	musical model of Brindisian gondola
FOURTH	cardigan or long combs
FIFTH	colander or tea-strainer
SIXTH	pottery carthorse
SEVENTH	small box to put things in or things to go in a small box
EIGHTH	garden ornament
NINTH	nether garment or nightshirt
TENTH	bobbin or sock
FIFTEENTH	Llamedosian spoon
TWENTIETH	stuffed donkey in straw hat
TWENTY-FIFTH	cooking apron with amusing anatomical design
THIRTIETH	lobster or crayfish
THIRTY-FIFTH	picture of sad green Agatean lady
FORTIETH	rabbit made from sea-shells
FORTY-FIFTH	teacosy
FIFTIETH	gold
FIFTY-FIFTH	four-poster bed
SIXTIETH	troll's tooth

Death

IT IS DEFINITELY very etiquette to mark the departure of some close friend or relative. If you go to their funerals, as we say in Lancre, they'll come to yours.

An important first step, though, is to make sure they're dead. It's amazin' how often people overlook this simple job, which can lead to much lack of etiquette and people havin' to run all the way back home from the graveyard to fetch a crowbar. But shouting 'Are you awake, Sid?' in their ear is not enough. In the Ramtops we organize a wake.

For those who don't know what a wake is, it's a bit like a birthday party only quite different. For one thing, no one is going to blow any candles out. Also, the requirement for jelly is seriously reduced. People can be quite cheerful at a wake, because it's not their wake. If the recently passed-away was popular, all their friends will come to pay their respects and give 'em a good send off, and if they're unpopular, everyone will turn up anyway to make sure they're dead. I advise lots of beer, and you can't go wrong with ham rolls. Some people like the coffin to be upright and open, but I think it is more etiquette to have it closed, especially if you are short of tables. Also, an open coffin can be a problem if people have had too much to drink, and are helping one another home and have got a bit short-sighted, because there's nothing more worrying to those tidyin' up than to find that the dear departed has

Death in his various forms comes to everything and everyone. (PS: We really meant that about the arsenic.)

160

really departed, and his old friends are halfway down the lane and wondering why he won't join in the singing.

An advantage to that, though, is that if the deceased is not dead, just sleeping, they might join the party, as happened over in Creel Springs when old Cable Volume woke up and asked for a pint and his friend Joe keeled over. Still, they had the beer and grub and a coffin all ready, hardly used, so it all turned out for the best, really.

In the big towns and cities things are a lot different.

I reckon that a long time ago, when people were walking around in skins and living in caves, someone dropped dead and while everyone was having a good cry someone shuffled up, presented his condolences, and said this week there was a special offer on shallow graves topped with cave bear skulls covered in ochre, and for only one big lump of mammoth extra there was also the option of having the grave lined with seasonal flowers. And so undertaking began. It is now very fashionable to be embalmed after you're dead, because the afterlife is uncertain and it may be possible to take it with you.

'GOING AWAY' PARTIES

ONE OF THE ADVANTAGES OF BEING A WITCH OR A WIZARD IS THAT YOU learn the time of your death in advance, and sometimes months before the big day. No one seems to know how this happens. Old witches I've spoken to say that one day you just wake up knowin', just like you can remember your birthday.

However it happens, it can be quite a saving in terms of buying new suits or starting any long books, and it is generally regarded as a good thing. After all, if you've lived a long time, and 100 is no age at all for a wizard or a witch, you're probably getting a bit bored and int'rested in seeing what happens next.

Wizards used to have 'going-away' parties, although I understand they don't happen much these days. They were a bit like wakes but with the principel guest still takin' an int'rest. I've heard stories that one or two wizards passed away from drinking or eating too much at their going-away parties, which raises very puzzlin' questions about Destiny, Fate, and so on. Generally it was all very good-humoured, especially if the wizard was really old, and a time for speeches and friendly recollections of times gone by.

Since wizards (and witches) can see Death, they always left out a glass of something and an extra plate of canapés in case he fancied a snack. You cannot go wrong with a ham roll.

For witches the 'knowledge' means that they can get their cottage really clean and an inventory done for the next occupier, because it'd be terrible to be dead knowing that you'd left things unswept. Traditionally they also dig their own graves and lie down in them towards the end, leaving the next witch to fill it in, because it is also not good manners to make more work than is necessary for other people.

Witches do not hold parties, although they do sometimes take tea with the other local witches to make sure that everything is handed over smoothly (you cannot go wrong with a ham roll). Also, over the years other witches will have had their eye on, as it might be, prized washstands and interestin'ly patterned basins and other items the soon-to-be-deceased might have accumulated, and it's much better to get this all sorted out beforehand. This prevents the other witches havin' to find excuses to nonchalantly enter the cottage afterwards, which can be particularly tricky if two do it at once. A true witch disdains any amount of fame and money, but will black someone's eye with the fender for a candlestick she's been coveting for thirty years. Many a spat involvin' quite serious magic has begun with the cry 'She promised it to me!'

As I have indicated, it is perfectly etiquettable to arrange your life so that everything ends cleanly, and a witch who dies just as the last log from the pile is smoulderin' in the hearth will get a reputation for being prudent as well as, of course, being dead.

What is not good manners is to tempt Fate. You might think that because you're not going to die for three months it might be fun to spend a few weeks climbing mountains, since it won't kill you, but there are no guarantees against accidents and in any case there is such a thing as a long and lingerin' death. The point is to wrap up all the loose ends neatly, which is as much as any person can hope for.

FLOWERS

MANY PEOPLE NOW SPECIFY 'NO FLOWERS' AND ASK INSTEAD FOR friends and more distant family to send donations of cash to a good cause, and in Lancre they ask for crockery for the wake, because a wake gets through a lot of crockery. I person'ly think that is sad. Flowers are a good tradition and one of the oldest there is. Of course they die off after a while, but then so do we all. That's the point, really.

PERIODS OF MOURNING

PEOPLE WORRY LESS ABOUT THIS SORT OF THING THAN THEY USED TO when I was young, when you bought a lot of black clothes around the age of forty and that was your wardrobe until all you needed was a shroud, and then I suppose at least the white made a change. I'm sorry to say that the tradition these days seems to be to avoid the close relatives for a few weeks out of embarrassment and then mumble something next time you can't avoid them.

That is the whole point about etiquette. It stops people having to flail around not knowin' what to do. It may be daft but at least there's some sort of rules which everyone understands.

When my fourth granddad died – my granny was a very good cook, and people came for miles around for her lard dumplings – my granny kept her curtains drawn for a week and it wasn't because of the effects of the wake. She also wore black for the rest of her life, but she'd been wearing black since she was thirty-five so that didn't make much difference. It used to be like that in those days; once your kids were grown up you got a sort of ment'l letter which said: You are an Old Person, and that was it. For a woman that meant a shawl and a bonnet was compuls'ry for the next sixty years, and the men would have to wear a grubby waist-coat and concertina trousers and take up an allotment.

I pinched this list of 'mourning periods' out of my granny's scrapbook. She was very keen on doing the right thing. Of course, in those days mourning and going to funerals and writin' letters of condolence and so on were quite a hobby for some people:

ONE MONTH	Friend's relatives
THREE MONTHS	Distant relatives (second cousins twice removed and so on)
SIX MONTHS	Closer relatives (uncles, cousins, etc)
ONE YEAR	In-laws, close friends
TWO YEARS	Very close relatives (immediate family)
THREE YEARS	Family pets (I see my granny has written in 'no goldfish')

No one seems to bother with these any more, but she also had rules for what the widow is supposed to wear. It makes you think.

First six months following death of husband:— Black only
Next three months:— Sombre grey may be added to the range
Three months to end of year one:— Grey can totally replace black
First six months of year two:— Purple may be added to the range
Second six months of year two:— Lavender may be added to the range
Year three:— It is now permissible to wear white clothes, if trimmed with black

I haven't even gone into the particulars about crêpe and silk, but it's pretty obvious that mourning was a full-time job. It doesn't actually say when the black edging stops or when she can get married again, but three years seems a long time to wait. If I'd waited three years I'd never have got anywhere. Person'ly I think black underwear is sufficient (provided it is meant to be black, of course; there are Standards, after all).

Husbands, on the other hand, wear mourning for only a couple of months. I find this very significant.

DEALING WITH THE UNDEAD

AT FIRST GLANCE THIS APPEARS VERY SIMPLE. NEARLY EVERYONE YOU meet is 'undead'. That's why they're called 'alive'.

But in fact we're talkin' about people who ought to be dead but ain't. They're mainly:

Vampires: the most troublesome kind of undead. This whole area has got a bit more difficult these days, what with vampires coming out of the casket and being more in-your-throat about what they do. Obviously, there's no book of etiquette at mealtimes. Here, however, are some sensible tips:

1 Don't go anywhere near a vampire's castle, no matter how bad the weather.
2 Having gone near the castle, don't knock at the huge forbidding door.
3 Having knocked at the huge forbidding door, don't accept the invitation from the strange man in black clothes to go inside.
4 Having gone inside, don't go into the guest bedroom.
5 Having gone into the guest bedroom, don't – whatever you do – sleep with the window open.
6 Having slept with the window open, don't come runnin' to me to complain.

Werewolves: and people say to me, werewolves aren't undead. Well, if you kill them without using fire or silver, you'll find them turning up again tomorrow. I can't think of a better word than 'undead'. Except possibly 'nuisance'.

Your pure-bred werewolf is gen'rally all right. When they're human, they act human, when they're a wolf, they act like a wolf. Except for their tendency to growl when they're annoyed and piss up against trees, you'd never know they was werewolves if you met 'em socially. Well . . . sometimes they have a tendency to . . . you know . . . sniff, but none of us is perfect.

If you are invited to dine, expect a lot of meat. And sometimes biscuits. Most of them love chocolate, so that is always a little gift worth taking along. Expect to go for a long walk in the afternoon.

Zombies: they're dead, but they won't lie down. No matter what people say, no one becomes a zombie unless they've got some very strong reason for staying alive, like some important task they have to finish. The proper etiquette is: since they're humans, treat them as human. It is not good manners to make cutting remarks like 'Isn't there something you should be doing? Like lying down?' and certainly not 'Decompose yourself.' They do appreciate little gifts of scent, aftershave and other strong-smelling items, and, believe me, you will want to give them these things.

Royal Occasions

IN MY EXPERIENCE people can tend to behave in an unnatural way when they find themselves in the presence of royalty. There is no need. Just remember they're only human; they all go to the toilet. Not when you go, of course. There are still some around who can have you put to death as soon as look at you, but mostly they just want to get through the day, they've seen people like you before, their wavin' hand is aching and if you do something daft you'll just get a tight little smile that'll haunt you for the rest of your life.

In Lancre we have what I suppose you'd call a constitutional monarchy if we had a constitution. What this means is this: there is only one king and more'n five hundred subjects, and they all work every day at jobs which mostly involve sharp things. It's one of those lessons that are so obvious they don't have to be taught.

It's all very fashionable these days for royalty to be accessible and busy itself with getting out and meetin' people. I think this is a bad idea. Politics is like chess, you need to know where the king and queen are all the time. There's nothing more annoying than doing a particul'y difficult roof and suddenly there's the Royal Family at the bottom of the ladder shouting up things like 'How long have you been a thatcher? How fascinating!' It's all very well sayin' royalty should do what the people want, but they'll want something different tomorrow.

MEETING ROYALTY

WHEN YOU ARE PRESENTED TO ROYALTY, NEVER SHAKE HANDS. Touching royalty is considered to be a gross intrusion. This is because royalty is contagious, and can rub off. That is why kings and queens wear gloves. Of course, this is only my opinion, but if you marry royalty you become royal and much more beautiful, if you're a woman, or more handsome, if you're a man, so there must be some reason. There's a magic to kings.

The King and Queen should be addressed, on first meeting, as 'Your Majesty'. Thereafter, they may be addressed either as 'Your Majesty' or as 'Sire' (for the King) or 'Ma'am' for the Queen. 'Ma'am' is pronounced to rhyme with 'ham', not with 'harm', These little touches make all the difference.

When talking to them, it is a good idea to avoid controversial subjects such as 'What about this republicanism, then? Is it a good idea or what?' and stick to general, unremarkable comments on the lines of 'If the ham in these sandwiches was cut any thinner I could see right through it.'

You should never refer to the King or Queen personally as 'you'. You should say, for example: 'I trust Your Majesty is enjoying the banquet'. Do not say 'There's plenty of meat left on that bone. Pass it here if you don't want it.' Rather say, 'If one does not wish to partake of one's gristle, one would be glad to take it off one's hands.'

Everyone knows that royalty traditionally does not carry money. However, it is not good etiquette to say, 'I can lend one a bob or two if one is short.'

TROOPING THE COLOUR

THIS IS A MAJOR CEREMONY IN THOSE KINGDOMS WHICH STILL HAVE an army and when you see all the pomp and stamping it's hard to remember that the whole purpose is just to show your average common soldier what his flag looks like.

Obviously you'd think they'd just know, but in the days when half your army were either prison scrapings or ploughboys who'd never seen a pair of trousers before, it was not always so easy. So 'Trooping the Colour' was invented to make sure everyone knew what their 'colours' looked like, so that they could recognize it in battle and return to it if commanded. There had been several embarrassing incidents where generals had been halfway home after a battle when they realized they had taken the wrong army, and this sort of thing can lead to bad feeling.

In Lancre, with an army of just one (Pte/Cpl/Sgt/C-in-C Ogg, S.), the flag is simply kept in the soldier's bunkhouse, so that, effectively, my boy Shawn performs the ceremony each time he goes to bed. It also acts as a handy extra blanket in cold weather. He knows it's the genuine Lancre flag when he sees it, because of the cocoa stains.

GARDEN PARTIES

KING VERENCE AND QUEEN MAGRAT LIKE TO HONOUR LOCAL worthies and visiting dignitaries by inviting them to garden parties held at Lancre Castle. Invitations are sent out by the Lord Chamberlain (Mr S. Ogg). These are fairly delicate affairs, where the strongest liquor available is tea and food consists of sandwiches containing a variety of non-animal-based products. Most Lancrastians try to ensure that they only attend one of the affairs.

This has led to a return of the traditional practice of royal invitations being considered to be 'commands'. By the royals, anyway.

INVESTITURES

THIS IS THE CEREMONY WHERE HONOURED CITIZENS COME TO receive awards of knighthoods or ironmongery for their services to the community. These can rank all the way up to a large house and a dukedom for life.

In Lancre it's all a bit more low key, but now we have the awards from OLE (Order of the Lancrastian Empire) for services to the Kingdom of Lancre (last presented to my son Shawn for his work in stopping draughts at the castle), down to a new set of Morris bells for being Lancrastian Dangerous Sports Personality of the Year.

We used to have knights and dames, but Lancre is a bit small for that sort of thing. I person'ly think the office of Dame could be re-introduced for any witches of a lit'rary inclination in the country, especially since I've already got a pair of spotted drawers and could always lay my hands on a goose if required.

What many people probably don't know is that when the sovereign dubs a knight by tapping him on the shoulders with a sword, it signifies that this is the last occasion when he can honourably be struck with a sword without returning the blow. There have been one or two occasions where recipients have forgotten this and which has led to some nasty scuffles.

If I have not got this wrong, this means that if you succeed in hitting a knight and running away quickly before he can fetch you a wallop, the King has to take his knighthood away from him.

Etiquette in the Bedroom

I REMEMBER MY OWN granny sayin' to me that a lady should always wear something in bed because it keeps a man int'rested, which is I why I gen'rally find it convenient to keep my hat on.

The whole issue of what I might call the nuptial side of marriage needs ~~~~~~ ~~~~~~ delicate etiquette goin'. When it comes to marit~~~~~~~~~~~~~~~~~~~~~~~~~~~~~~~~~~~~ Aunt Harriet had a woo~~~~~~ it came ~~~~~~ dry uncl~~~~~~ he sno~~~~~~ it real~~~~~~ they trie~~~~~~ of an enormous thing power~~~~~~~~~~~~~~~~~~~~~~~~~~~~ old trick of sewing a ball on the back of his nigh~~~~~~~ him sleeping on his back, but he could do it in any position. People say to me, what about the couple sleeping in separate beds, and I say 'It depends on whose they are'. Now you can get them ~~~~~~ t ~~ ~~~~~~ ~

> **Memo from J.H.C. Goatberger**
> **To: Thos. Cropper, overseer**
>
> I have to tell you that my wife found the proofs of this section. I could hear her laughing two rooms away. Since when she has given me some very odd looks. I thought you told me that this book was devoid of bad language?

> **Memo from Thos. Cropper**
> **To: J.H.C. Goatberger, publisher**
>
> I have personally looked up every word in the dictionary. I believe the problem is that Mrs Ogg can do things with perfectly innocent words that most people require very explicit language to achieve.

~~~~~~~~~~~~~~ pick up the general idea, b~~~~ ~~~~~~ said 'animal husbandry' is an unfortunate term, but maybe not as bad as 'going to bed with the chickens'. To my mind pink fluffy slippers won't be any help. She had a wig and a glass

eye, too, but she had four hus_____ and
tha_____ pen-
mi_____ ping
one_____ loor
nev_____ Of
cou_____ bedrooms were a
diffe_____ place in those days, and you had the goat tied to the
bedpost the family were in there

> **Memo from J.H.C. Goatberger**
> To: Thos. Cropper, overseer
>
> You mean the bit about the socks?

buy
obv
whe
the
mon
ter e

> **Memo from Thos. Cropper**
> To: J.H.C. Goatberger, publisher
>
> I was referring to the bit about carpet slippers.
> I think the bit about socks is just about socks.

that pillo_____ fine weather it was different, there_____ had to
cough po_____ phrase
'more si_____ avourite
tree. He _____ a really
deep fea_____ n to her
leg, othe_____ ch party.
It's reall_____ n what a
woman _____ man is a
clean a_____ vs what's
she's do_____ keep an
oven hot, and cooking_____ you get.
Coquettes don't last, but courgettes are nice with cheese.

> **Memo from J.H.C. Goatberger**
> To: Thos. Cropper, overseer
>
> Oh, no . . . I've just re-read the bit about
> slippers, and when I mentioned it to my wife
> she said, 'Of course.' And it's all written in
> perfectly innocent words, such as might be
> used by children and unmarried women. All
> this section is to be deleted. There is to be
> no argument.

I think that if everyone was to follow these few simple rules,
there would be more love in the world.

AFTERWORD

I T IS MY hope, as I approach the twilight of my years, or at least the afternoon tea, that some of this information will be of use to those people who look on me as a beacon of rectitude an' knowledge.

I have tested the recipes and hardly any of them make you throw up. As for the etiquette, well, I have done my best. Life is full of little tricks and if you're allowed to go around again, well, they don't let you take the notes you made the first time. I hope my efforts will provide you with a sketch map.

But really, etiquette is a state of mind. You never know what tomorrow will bring. It might hold a problem no one has yet had to face. So therefore you need to get your mind right for when you venture into areas where no book is going to help you. Remember: someone had to be the first person in the world to eat an oyster.

In that case, my advice is to try a nice open smile, although this admittedly won't get you far with shellfish. I do find it gets me out of trouble with people nine times out of ten, and even if it does get me into trouble it's generally int'resting trouble and leads to warm memories. You couldn't buy them for money.

Gytha Ogg
'Tir Nani Ogg', The Square, Lancre